Alix peered into the mirror. It was pretty weird to suddenly have short hair, but she had to admit it didn't look all that bad. And then Stacy got up and came over and stood next to her. They both looked in the mirror and had the same thought.

"Far out," Stacy whispered. "We look exactly alike. No one in the world could tell us apart now."

Alix nodded and said under her breath, "It's going to work. We're really going to pull this off."

**Other Apple Paperbacks
you will enjoy:**

The Secret Diary of Katie Dinkerhoff
by Lila Perl

No Place for Me
by Barthe DeClements

I Thought You Were My Best Friend
by Ann Reit

Sixth Grade Secrets
by Louis Sachar

You, Me, and Gracie Makes Three
by Dean Marney

Twin Switch

Carol Stanley

AN
APPLE
PAPERBACK

SCHOLASTIC INC.
New York Toronto London Auckland Sydney

ISBN 0-590-44617-7

12 11 10 9 8 7 6 5 4 3 2 1   0 1 2 3 4 5/9

Printed in the U.S.A.   01

First Scholastic printing, May 1989

For Lyn DelliQuadri

Chapter 1

Outside the classroom window, it was a spectacular June afternoon, with the last of the desert wildflowers shimmering red and blue on the foothills. Stacy Wyatt didn't see any of this and wouldn't have been able to appreciate it even if she had. She was too deep in misery.

She stared down at the geometry problem on the test in front of her. She didn't have a clue to the answer, or even on how to begin figuring it out. Geometry made her feel dumb, even though she was sure she wasn't, not really. She had a lot of ideas about a lot of things. They just weren't usually school things.

Stacy looked around the room. Most of the class had finished the exam and were already gone. The only ones still there besides Stacy were Felicia Hart (known around school as "Earth to Felicia"), who was now staring out the window, enjoying the beautiful day, and Paul Durkin, who was furiously erasing everything he'd just done. The linoleum floor around his desk was covered with eraser lint.

Tap, tap, tap. Mr. Henley was knocking his pencil on the edge of the desk. The five-minute warning. Stacy looked back down at the question on the isosceles triangle, sighed with the hopelessness of it all and got up. Might as well just bag it.

Outside in the hall, Stacy's boyfriend, Sam, was waiting, hacking around with Jason. The two of them were taking long drinks from the water fountain, then chasing and trying to spray each other. Stacy stood watching for a moment. She just loved how Sam looked. She thought he was probably the cutest guy at Joshua Tree High — so rugged and blond and tan, kind of like a surfer, although their town was on the edge of the Mojave desert, miles and miles from the ocean. Then Sam saw Stacy.

"Human squirt guns," he said, swallowing and laughing as Jason took him by surprise and squirted a long stream of water down the back of his shirt.

"And *I* was worried about seeming stupid," Stacy said sarcastically.

"Being last one out of one of Henley's finals is stupid," Sam teased, putting his arm around her. "Playing human squirt gun is only *im-mature*." He waved good-bye to Jason, who dropped back and nodded and walked off down the hall. Stacy and Sam were a couple and Jason was giving them their space. Around Joshua Tree High, couples were a big deal. It was a lot better to be in one, even if, like Stacy, you weren't quite sure you were in a couple with the right person.

"So how'd you do, do you think?" Sam asked Stacy when they were crossing the school lawn to the parking lot.

"Horrible, of course," she said. "If I got anything right, it was an accident. Looks like summer school for me if I'm going to get to be a junior next fall," Stacy said. "Although I don't know what good summer school will do. It'll just be the same stuff, only the kids'll be all the dumb ones and the classroom will be hotter and Mr. Henley's fuse will be shorter."

"Does this mean you won't be able to go on the Wilderness Trek?" Sam said. The school trek, this year through Yosemite National Park in the northern part of the state, was the best part of summer vacation for all the kids in Joshua Tree who were outdoor freaks, and this included most of Stacy and Sam's friends.

"Afraid not," Stacy said, shaking her head. "Summer school starts the first week in July, the same time as the trek. You'll have to go without me."

"It'd be better if you could manage to come."

"But I just told you, I'm going to have to go to summer school. Which is more important — that I make it into eleventh grade, or that I go on the wilderness trek so you can have a date?"

Sam actually stopped for a second to consider the question. Stacy couldn't believe it.

"Well," he finally said. "It'd just be good if you could do both." He was pouting!

"Hey," she said, trying to bring him around, "look on the bright side. This way you can hang out with Jason and the guys more. Take the easier trails. This time I won't be there to show you up, let everyone know what a wimp you really are."

Teasing Sam that he was a secret wimp was a running joke between them, one which Sam could handle easily, seeing as he was the star defensive lineman on the Joshua Tree Coyotes. Still, when they ran together and she beat him, he didn't really like it, which didn't stop Stacy from beating him, but did add another edge to their relationship.

"Come on," he said now, getting in behind the wheel of his old beat-up VW Beetle. "Jason's got the new Squeeze tape. We can go over to his place and hang out. You can watch us play pool."

"Great," Stacy said, and then hoped he hadn't heard the sarcasm in her voice. What she really wanted to do was go running by herself. She'd missed her chance that morning before school, when she was still hopelessly cramming for the stupid geometry test. A good long run through the foothills outside of town would be just the thing to blow away the crummy feelings she had about the test and herself. A run would also give her some time alone to think about how she was going to tell her mother that she was flunking geometry.

But the other guys would be bringing their girlfriends over to Jason's, and Sam would want Stacy to be there, too. This was kind of flattering but also kind of a pain.

She stayed at Jason's for an hour or so, watching Sam play pool, shouting encouragement from the sidelines, being quiet when he was about to make a crucial shot, saying "all right" when he sunk one. Standard girlfriend duties. Mostly though, she talked with her friend, Rosalie. Rosalie went with Mike Beals, who was generally acknowledged to be the coolest guy in the whole school, both the best-looking and the best personality. Stacy thought Mike was just a great person, nice to everyone, the kind of guy you expected to go off and do some great good for the world.

Rosalie — in spite of being kind of a goofball, and quite a bit overweight, and having the largest bunch of braces ever installed in a single mouth — acted like having Mike as a boyfriend was no particular big deal. Her attitude was precisely what kept him wound around her little finger. Sometimes Stacy couldn't believe how primitive boys were.

"Got a letter from Alix yesterday," Stacy told Rosalie when they were settled in on the big old velvet sofa in the corner of Jason's family room. Alix was Stacy's twin sister. She lived with their father in Chicago. Stacy missed her like crazy.

They were identical twins. Not only did they look alike, with the same auburn hair and fair skin and green eyes, but they were alike *inside*, too. Not that they had the same interests — not by a long shot. Stacy was super-athletic, while Alix's idea of exercise was reading a heavy book. Alix was straight A's in school, while Stacy had to work to keep up a C+ average. Alix was one of the most promising violinists at the music conservatory, while Stacy had been asked to please *not* sing "The Star-Spangled Banner" before school games because she threw everyone else off key. Of course, where Stacy had Alix beat by a mile was with people. Although she'd only been out here in California two years, she was one of the most popular girls in school. Alix, on the other hand, was so shy she hardly had any friends at all.

But in spite of all these differences, the twins both felt that in the really important ways, on the deepest levels, they were very much alike. They called it their "affinity." For instance, when they talked to each other, they usually didn't have to finish their sentences. When they lived together, even though they had separate rooms and got dressed by themselves, they usually showed up at breakfast wearing the same color. When they were little, they amazed people with their number game. One would pick a number between one and ten, then close her eyes and think of it. The other twin could always guess it.

"You got the letter with you?" Rosalie asked now, absently winding three long strands of her blonde hair into a braid.

"Mmm," Stacy said, pulling it out of the back pocket of her ice-washed jeans. She unfolded it and read,

Dear Stace,

Guess what? I made first chair in the violin section of the conservatory orchestra! I can hardly believe it. I was sure Bobby Zacek was going to beat me out. Dad and Martine took me to dinner at Ambria to celebrate. Very fancy, my dear. They bring out your dinner on a plate, but under a silver dome and then lift it in front of you. Voilà! I had shrimp something. It was great. I wish I could say as much for the company. Dad and Martine are still in teen love. At one point they actually held hands across the table. I could have died.

I really don't know what to talk about with her. I mean she's not my mother and she's not my friend. I stay in my room a lot. At least I'm getting a ton of reading done. At the moment, I'm reading *War and Peace*. Two guesses what it's about.

Hope you get through your geometry test all right. You will, I know. There are really only a couple of tricky parts to geometry and the rest of it's cinchy stuff like the isosceles triangle.

See you at grandma's. Can't wait.

Love,
Alix

"You two going to your grandmother's farm?" Rosalie asked.

Stacy nodded.

"Soon as school's out. I can't wait. I haven't seen her since Easter."

"I wish I didn't have to see *my* sister until *next* Easter."

"Your sister is the worst person we know. She wakes your parents up at night to point out that you're coming in late. She rings the doorbell and tells you it's someone to see you, then steals your place on the couch *and* eats your sandwich. *My* sister, on the other hand, is wonderful. Besides, she's my twin. If I don't see her for too long, I get . . . I don't know . . . lonely is too weak a word. More like I'm missing some part of myself."

"Nothing personal," Rosalie said. This was how she started off all sentences that were going to contain something personal and insulting. "But I think twins are weird. You're out here and your sister's in Chicago so that you can break free of twin weirdness. So that you can develop independent personalities."

"That's just what one dopey child psychologist said. Unfortunately, he was the one my parents picked to take us to. They really ought to have shrinks for twins who are twins themselves. *They'd* understand."

Rosalie nodded, but Stacy could see she'd already drifted off the subject. She was watching the guys play.

"Sam sure is cute," she said.

"You think?" Stacy said, fishing for a compliment, but Rosalie was on her own track.

"You know something really neat about the two of you?"

"What?" Stacy said. She'd like to know something neat about her and Sam. Lately nothing about them seemed especially neat.

"Your names go together. Stacy and Sam. Sam and Stacy. Kind of like name karma, if you think about it."

Stacy rolled her eyes. It was pretty typical of Rosalie's insights on life, though. And *she* passed geometry!

Sam was deep into the pool game when Stacy got up to leave.

"So soon?" he said, even though he hadn't spent a second with her since they'd gotten there.

"I've got to get home and fix dinner."

"Uh, oh, okay." He pulled her toward him and gave her a kiss. "I'll call tonight!" he shouted up the stairs after her. "At seven." This was to make sure she was waiting by the phone. He didn't like it when her mother answered and he had to make small talk to get through to Stacy.

When Stacy got home — the third in a bank of ten identical stuck-together town houses on the edge of town — she tossed her stuff in the front hall closet and scooped the cat up with one hand.

"Sushi, you sweet thing. How's about some liver bits?"

"Murf," said Sushi. He'd been an alley kitten who'd lost his mother too soon and had never learned a proper meow. Murf was the best he could do.

Stacy opened a can of cat food while Sushi rubbed around her ankles in anticipation. After she'd put the cat's food out, Stacy looked around for the hamburger she was sure she'd set out to defrost this morning.

"Oh, no," she said aloud when she opened the freezer and saw it still up there, glistening frostily at her. "Going to have to get creative."

By the time her mother came home from work, dinner was ready.

"Mmm," Karen Wyatt said as she came through the back door, sniffing at the aroma from the stove. "What's for dinner?"

"Hot dog and cottage cheese omelet ranchero," Stacy said.

Her mother burst out laughing. "Sounds like the day before the day we absolutely have to do the grocery shopping," she said.

"It might be good," Stacy said, trying to persuade herself.

"Of course it'll be good. I don't think you've ever made anything bad. *Weird* maybe — but never bad. Let me just put my stuff away."

"You want to eat in front of the TV?" Stacy asked.

"No, let's stay here. I've got something I want to discuss with you."

The geometry test! Stacy thought. Henley called her mother at work. But when they'd sat down across from each other at the little dinette table, her mother didn't seem mad or upset at all. First she just pointed into the black plastic bowl and asked, "What's this?"

"Tomato, orange, asparagus, and peanut salad," Stacy said.

Her mother nodded. "I need your advice."

"Shoot," Stacy said.

"I've been asked out on a date."

"You have? Who?" Stacy said, a little too loud, choking a little on a piece of asparagus.

"Well, it's not *that* astonishing, is it?"

"Oh, no, I mean . . . well . . . it's just that — "

"Just that *what*?"

"Well, you don't *go* out on dates."

"Well, I haven't, it's true. For a long time after your father and I split up, I wasn't interested. And then for another while I didn't see anyone who seemed interesting enough to go through the trouble for."

"And now you have? Who is this guy?" Stacy could hear the hostile tone in her own voice and was surprised at herself. Why was she so unsettled by her mother having a date?

"His name is Alan. Alan Sakamoto."

"Sakamoto?"

"Yes, he's Japanese-American."

Stacy nodded, but didn't say anything. Her mother held her fork in mid-air, a bit of omelet sitting on it and peered across at her daughter.

"You don't have any secret prejudice against Japanese people that I don't know about, do you?"

"Oh, no, nothing like that. I was just picturing how oddly people will look at us when he's my stepfather."

"Stacy! Stop it. I'm having one little date with a nice guy I just met, and you've already got me at the altar. Give me — as you would say — a break!"

"Okay," Stacy said, looking down at her food, feeling awful for hassling her mother, who hardly ever got out and had any fun. For a minute she just sat there like that, thinking what a crummy daughter she was. And then — out of the blue — the weirdest, funniest thought struck her, and she burst out laughing in the middle of the dead, silent kitchen.

"What?" her mother said.

"I was just thinking," Stacy said, but was laughing so hard she couldn't get it out at first. Finally she was able to finish her sentence. "What are we going to do about the cat?"

"What do you mean?" her mother asked.

"Well, Sushi is kind of an odd name for an animal. Do you think it looks like we're making fun of Japanese food?"

"Oh, boy, I don't know," she said. "Maybe you're right. Maybe, to be on the safe side, when he's here, we should just call her Sue."

The notion of calling the cat — who was a male in the first place — Sue, set them both off laughing, and Stacy decided not to ruin a perfectly nice moment by bringing up the sad story of her career in geometry.

Chapter 2

"Bellissima!" Professor Faraci said as Alix played the final notes of the concerto and lifted her bow from the strings of her violin.

She beamed with satisfaction. She'd been working on this ending all week, and it looked like she'd gotten it right. Professor Faraci was a strict teacher, not exactly lavish with praise. When he said *"Bellissima!"* it was like anyone else saying "Far out!"

"Alix," he said now as she was gently nestling her violin into the blue velvet lining of its leather case. "I must be telling you something. I am going away for the summer. Back to Italy. My mother, she is very old and not well. I am thinking it is good to make her a visit before . . ." He left the sentence dangling. Alix tried to hide her astonishment. She never thought of Professor Faraci having a mother.

He was already the oldest person she knew, older than her grandmother. If he had a mother she must be a hundred.

"But what'll I do without you?" she said, pulling her sheet music off the stand.

"I was thinking maybe you could study under Taylor. He is — "

Alix put up her hand.

"No. Please. I don't want to study with Taylor, or anyone else. You're the best violin coach in the city, one of the best in the world. Working under someone else would just feel like standing in place after years of flying."

Faraci smiled and ran his hands through his curly gray hair.

"All right. Then we will make a plan for working through the concerti we had in the line."

"Lined up," she corrected his English.

"Yes. You will have to practice on your alone."

"On my own," Alix said. "Well, I'll try. But it won't be the same."

"Oh, this I know," Professor Faraci said. He was not modest about his stature as a violin teacher.

Alix walked down the musty staircase of the conservatory thinking about Professor Faraci, then about herself. She was happy at her musical progress, but gloomy about the state of her social life. What kind of fifteen-year-old was she anyway? Basically, her best friend was her old Italian violin coach. Why didn't she have friends her own age? Why didn't she have a boyfriend? She knew the answers. It was all because she was the shyest person in the world. It was the curse of her life.

She came out the old front doors of the conservatory into a ferocious early summer storm. Rain was shooting down like wet bullets on the wide sidewalk. She pushed her umbrella open against it and put her violin inside the front of her cotton jacket, resigning herself to getting completely drenched as she crossed Michigan Avenue to wait for her bus. Why is it, she thought, that just when you're already feeling miserable inside, it always starts raining, too?

Finally — after about ten wrong buses — hers came along. She climbed up the steep steps and slid her dollar into the little machine next to the driver.

"Step to the rear!" he shouted, and everyone shifted a little, but didn't really move. Almost everyone was smashed together in the front part of the bus. Because they'd all been waiting forever in the rain for this bus, they were all damp. And because the bus's heating system was on full-blast — in spite of it being June — it was like being inside a steam bath. At moments like this, Alix absolutely hated living in a big city and envied Stacy living in a nice small town in California, where she didn't have to take a bus anywhere. Where it hardly ever rained. And where she didn't have to go home to face Martine, the Wicked Stepmother.

Actually, there wasn't anything really wicked about Martine, except that she'd married Steve Wyatt, Alix's father. And even that wasn't really wicked. It wasn't as though she'd stolen him away from Alix's mother, like in some tacky soap opera subplot. They'd already been divorced a couple of years when he started seeing Martine.

Still, Martine being married to Alix's father seemed weird, too weird for Alix to cope with. Martine was only twenty-eight. Alix's father was forty. It was impossible for Alix to relate to Martine like she was some kind of parent. And they didn't have anything in common, so she couldn't relate to her like she was some kind of older sister. About the only way she *could* relate to Martine was hating her, and wishing she would go away, leaving her father free to go back and marry her mother. Which is what Alix wanted more than almost anything in the world.

Maybe Martine would be out when she got home. Maybe she had a flight today and would be gone until tomorrow. Martine was a flight attendant, and those nights she was laying over in some other city, Alix got her dad all to herself. They'd go out to the video store and rent a movie and watch it together over a dinner of microwave cheeseburgers and microwave popcorn. Maybe that's what they'd do tonight. Alix crossed her fingers.

"Hi, Edward," she said to the doorman as she came into her building, an old high-rise facing the park.

"Hello, Alix," he said, tipping his hat. Edward was a pretty strange-looking doorman. He was the last of the hippies, with a walrus mustache and a pony tail sticking out from under his doorman's hat. Alix always imagined that on his days off he hung out around his house in bellbottoms and a tie-dyed T-shirt, playing his old Bob Dylan albums. "How's the rock and roll going?" He nodded toward her violin. He liked to tease her that she was a secret rock star, that there was really an electric guitar inside her case.

"Great. I was just working through a few new numbers with Sting. Say, did Martine by any chance leave on a trip today?"

Edward shook his head.

"Don't know. Haven't seen her all day."

Alix's spirits lifted. Maybe . . .

She rode up in the panelled elevator, got out on sixteen and let herself into the apartment. She stood in the foyer for a moment listening. Nothing. Absolute silence. Maybe Martine *had* left town after all. Her hopes soared. She put down her violin and briefcase and began walking back through the hallway, taking a look in the living room, the dining room, the den — all empty. She didn't even bother looking in the kitchen. Martine didn't cook. Alix's bedroom door was shut. The bathroom was open and empty. Only one more place to check. She practically rushed into the master bedroom, sure that she was in luck, that Martine was winging her way to Omaha or San Francisco or Miami, standing in the aisle of some plane demonstrating an oxygen mask.

She peered into the bedroom. And it did look empty at first glance. But then came a voice from the floor on the other side of the bed.

"Hello, Alix." Martine sat up, stretching like a cat. "Just doing my yoga. How was your day?"

"Fine," Alix said in a zombie voice (Alix the Undead) she'd perfected for speaking to Martine. She stood in the doorway and watched as Martine went over to the mirrored dressing table across from the bed, picked up her spray bottle of rose water and misted her face. She called this "hydrating" her skin, and did it several times a day. Martine worried about her skin. She thought she was already getting wrinkles, even though Alix couldn't see them.

"When's Dad getting home?" Alix asked now.

"Oh, he's already been here. He went out to pick up some dinner. Thai carryout. Should be back any minute. Why don't you go wash those hands before we eat? You look like you could stand a little freshening up."

"Right," Alix the Undead said. She hated it when Martine said motherly things like "Why don't you go wash your hands?" It was so fake. She went to her room and deliberately did not wash up. She flipped on her boom box and Beethoven came up loud on the speakers. She threw herself on the bed and felt something crinkly underneath her. She rolled over. It was a letter, from Stacy.

"Oh, great," Alix said softly to herself as she dug her little finger under the flap and ripped open the envelope and smiled as she saw the typical one huge paragraph of tiny, cramped, almost illegible script.

Hey Twin,

I know this will absolutely astonish you, but I managed to flunk geometry. Do you think it's possible that when we were in the womb together, all the brain cells went into *your* head? It's the only way I can account for this dismal state of affairs, which now includes my going to summer school. The only thing in my immediate life that I have to look forward to is meeting you at Gram's. That is, if you're still coming. If you can *bear* to leave Martine for two weeks. I know you'll miss her terribly, but I'll try to cheer you up. See you sooooon! And hey — congrats on getting that first chair in the orchestra. Is it a better chair? I imagine it covered in rose-colored velvet.

Identically yours,
Stacy

"News from Sis?" Martine said, standing in Alix's doorway. She always referred to Stacy as "Sis." It drove Alix crazy.

"Nothing special," she said in her zombie voice. She folded the letter and put it in the pocket of her skirt. "Dad back yet?"

"Just got here," Martine said. "Come on in and eat."

Alix waited until Martine had left the room. Then she went over to the window, reached out and rubbed her hands around in the soot on the sill. Not the most mature thing to do, she knew, but it felt great.

"You must be getting excited — about going down to Gram's," Steve Wyatt said, passing a carton of beef and broccoli across the table. "I hear Nellie foaled this spring. You'll get to see the new colt."

Alix nodded.

"Gram's waiting for me and Stace to get there to name it. She wanted to call it Biscuits, but we told her that's a name for a cat, and so she's going to hold off." Alix stopped and remembered to ask, "Did you get my plane ticket?"

Her father nodded. He was pulling a cashew out of one of the open cartons with his chopsticks. He ate with chopsticks about as well as a Chinese person. He could also do a jackknife dive off a high board. He could get a kite up in the air even when there was hardly any wind. He was, in Alix's opinion, just an all-around terrific person.

Alix never really understood why he and her mother had split up. Her mom had said it was because he was too into his career — advertising account exec — and not into the family enough. In that way, Alix supposed Martine was probably a better person for him. She was gone about half the time flying around the country. And she didn't cook, so she was never mad when he was late for dinner. She looked up now and saw her father brushing away a blonde, frizzy curl off Martine's forehead.

Barf, Alix thought. The lovebirds are at it again. Whenever they acted like this in front of her, she couldn't help thinking they wished she wasn't here. Well, in a week, she wouldn't be. She'd be far away, down in Missouri with Gram and Stacy and a colt that was *not* going to be named Biscuits.

Chapter 3

Stacy got off the plane and went into the St. Louis terminal. The waiting area was full of people. She stopped and looked around. No Gram, no Alix. Where could they be? Could they have just completely forgotten her?

She stared enviously at all the other passengers getting warm greetings and big hugs from their friends and families, and suddenly felt very alone. Then, in the middle of all the other voices, she could hear two calling out her name.

"Stacyyy!"

And there were Gram and Alix, running like crazy down the corridor toward her. How could she have forgotten that her grandmother was *never* on time? The family always joked that she'd be late for her own funeral.

"We started out ever so early, I'll have you know," Gram was already rushing in to explain, before she'd even said hello. "But then all of a sudden, there on Route 66 there was this huge flea market. I'd never seen it before. It just sort of rose up off the side of the highway. Like a mirage. We couldn't resist."

At this point, Alix was pointing sideways at her grandmother, to show Stacy it was *Gram* who hadn't been able to resist. Gram shushed her and kept right on with her rush of explanation.

"We got us an old weather vane you won't believe."

"You mean to go with the forty-seven other weather vanes you got at all those other fabulous flea markets?" Stacy teased.

"I think the flea market guys see your old truck coming, Gram," Alix added. "They say to each other, 'Run quick and haul out all those old weather vanes. Here comes that crazy Nora Wyatt!'"

Gram smiled and hugged them both. She always took their teasing well, which was good, because the twins were big on teasing.

"All right, all right," Gram admitted, "so I have a harmless weakness for weather vanes. Give an old lady a break. And come on with you both. Let's go fetch Stacy's bags and get a move on. Time's a-wasting!"

"Gram's going to take us out to the Old Wind-mill for a picnic," Alix told Stacy.

"All right!" said Stacy, who loved the Old Windmill better than just about any place else on earth.

As they walked down to the baggage claim, Stacy looked over at her sister and saw that she was wearing a pink polo shirt and a denim skirt. Stacy wasn't surprised. She herself had on a pink cotton sweater and jeans. Unless the twins checked with each other first to make sure they *didn't* wear the same colors, they always did. It was just one of the eerie connections between them.

Another was how much they looked alike. Exactly, to be exact. Stacy always felt a momentary shock when she saw her sister after these long absences. It was always a little surprising to come face to face with her mirror image. The same long, thin nose, the same tall willowy build, the same green eyes, the same tiny gap between the front teeth. They even had the same small birthmark on their right arms. Except for the fact that Stacy wore her curly auburn hair short and Alix kept hers shoulder length, nobody — except themselves — could tell the two of them apart.

Stacy had heard that everyone in the world

had a twin somewhere, but hers was right here. Sometimes this seemed like the most wonderful piece of luck; other times it seemed pretty weird — like having a double, another her, but *not* her. Sometimes she and Alix talked about this kind of stuff — twin stuff — but not lately. Lately, separated by two thousand miles, they hardly got to talk at all.

"You've already been here a day?" she asked Alix now.

"Two. I wanted to get the jump on you so I could eat all of Gram's raspberry preserves and name the colt and have the first swim in the quarry without you."

For a split second, Stacy believed her sister, then saw a smile start at the corners of Alix's mouth and knew her sister was pulling her leg.

"Well, then, I might as well take the next flight back to California. Seeing as I've already missed all the fun."

"Oh, why don't you come on the picnic with me and Gram? I think we saved a crust of a sandwich or something for you. And Jake'll give you some of his dog food."

Jake was waiting for them, resting his head in the open window of the cab of Gram's old pickup truck.

"See," Gram said. "He's happy to see you, Stacy. He's smiling." While Stacy would've died of embarrassment trying to explain to anyone out in California that her grandmother had a dog that smiled, it was an undeniable fact that Jake grinned just like a person when he was happy. And he was grinning from one long ear to the other at the moment as he leaned out the window to greet her.

"Dogs in the back!" Gram yelled as she opened the door. Jake obediently jumped down out of the cab and ran around and hopped into the bed of her truck. The twins followed, hoisting themselves up on the back bumper and jumping in, bringing Stacy's bags with them as they flopped down on the piled up feed sacks. They both loved to ride in the back of the truck.

"Here we go!" Gram shouted as she started up the truck with a rumble and a roar and a blast of exhaust. And off they went, the girls getting tossed around the back with every little bump in the road. They didn't care. It was a sunny summer day, and they were heading down into the country that was a part of their childhood and was now the only place where they got to be together.

After a while, the truck turned off the main highway onto an old two-lane, then further along, onto a gravel country road. Then, just before they would've hit Cordelia — the town closest to Gram's farm — they turned off onto a little hidden lane covered with the overhanging branches of trees. The twins had to scrunch way down to avoid getting brushed by leaves. They were almost at the Old Windmill.

They got their first glimpse of it as they came over a ridge. There it was, as ever. They'd been coming here since they were little girls. They'd changed in a million ways, but the Old Windmill was exactly the same — made of stone, with a red roof and behind it, the fast-running brook. Gram fishtailed through the gravel lot next to the mill (she didn't drive like anybody's grandmother they knew) and pulled to a stop.

The twins hopped out as Gram hauled the old wicker picnic basket down from the cab of the truck. They helped her. Jake acted like he wanted to help.

"You don't suppose he could be interested in those ham sandwiches inside, do you?" Gram said, waving him away. "Come on," she said to the twins. "Race you to the bank." This was Gram's backward way of saying the two of them should go on ahead. She and Jake were both a little old and slow and would take their time.

"Give us the basket, Gram," Alix said.

"Yeah, we'll have the picnic all set up by the time you get there," Stacy added.

Each of them took a handle and swung the basket between them as they walked down to the soft, grassy bank of the brook.

"It's so great to be here!" Stacy said as they set the basket down and began spreading an old threadbare blanket. "I feel like lying down and hugging the grass."

"Don't do that. Gram will think you've gone completely weird, instead of just a little weird, which she already knows you are. Come on. Let's set up the picnic. Let's be perfect granddaughters — for a change."

They opened the lid of the picnic basket and pulled out a foil-wrapped plate. Stacy peeked inside.

"Fried chicken."

"Ham sandwiches," Alix said, inspecting one.

"Oh, great. From Gram's smokehouse. Mmmm. What's this?" Stacy opened a freezer carton. "Ah. Potato salad."

"Chocolate layer cake," Alix said, opening the top of a covered cake plate to show Stacy.

"Homemade?"

"Of course. We baked it this morning."

"Oh, look!" Stacy exclaimed. "Gram even put in a treat for our four-legged furry friend." She unwrapped and held up a large marrow bone. And right on cue, Jake loped by and snatched the bone. Clutching it in his dog jaws (and still grinning a dog grin), he found a place nearby and began munching as Gram got to the blanket and sat down.

"Boy, you two really got this meal out in record time. And I'm ready — hungry as a horse."

"Are horses really that hungry?" Stacy teased. "Or is that just another one of those exaggerated farm expressions? Like knee-high to a grasshopper?"

"What about corn being as high as an elephant's eye?" Alix joined in. "I mean, do they actually bring an elephant out to Missouri and check the corn against it?"

By this time they had Gram laughing.

"The fact is that it's pretty darn boring during farm winters," she said. "Two months of feeding the chickens and fixing the harnesses. That takes up December and January. By February farmers have finished off every possible chore and so they usually just devote the month to making up ridiculous exaggerated farm expressions. It's a rural tradition. Which I'm passing on to you. You should be properly grateful. Now pass that chicken and tell me how things are going with the two of you — twinwise, that is."

Gram was a twin herself. Her sister Sarah lived in Kansas City with her husband, but the two of them talked nearly every day on the phone. Gram had been against splitting the twins up — and sympathized with their loneliness for each other these past three years.

"Not so great," Stacy said. "And now Mom and Dad're mad at the long distance bills."

"Well, I can understand that. Sarah and I are always mad at *ourselves* for our long distance bills. It's a problem. Did you start keeping journals for each other like I suggested?"

Both girls nodded.

"We'll show each other while we're here at the farm."

"I'd love to see those journals," Gram teased.

"No way!" Stacy said emphatically.

"You could read mine," Alix said. "Isn't that pitiful? Fifteen and I'm leading such a boring life I could show my diary to my grandmother!"

"Oh, I'll bet you've got some juicy gripes about poor Martine," Gram said.

"*Poor* Martine," Alix said sarcastically. "She tried to hug me good-bye in the train station. I pretended I had to tie my shoe instead."

"You're so hard on her," Stacy said.

"Easy for you to say."

"I know, I know. I don't have to live with her. Oh, I didn't have a chance to write you this — Mom may have a new boyfriend."

"Really? Have you met him?"

Stacy nodded.

"Alan Sakomoto. He's Japanese-American."

"Is he nice?" Gram said.

"Oh, yeah. And he owns two record stores — that's his business. So he brought me a couple of albums. Psychedelic Furs and U2. That was just his guess. Not bad. And he asked what I really like, so he can bring more later."

"Oh, no," Alix said, "If Mom marries him, then there's even less hope for her and Dad getting back together."

Stacy looked hard at her sister, handed her a ham sandwich and said, "There's *no* hope. None. You might have noticed that Dad's remarried. Sometimes you act like Martine doesn't really exist, like she's just on some TV show you see at your house. She's Dad's *wife*! I mean, like her or not, you've got to get real about this."

Alix looked to her grandmother for support, but Gram only said, "I'm afraid Stacy's right. However you feel about her, it seems that Mar-

tine's going to be on the scene for a while."
Gram paused here, then added in an odd
tone of voice, "What with one thing, and another . . ."

"What one thing?"

"What other?"

The twins knew their grandmother was holding something back.

"Well, I probably shouldn't be spilling the
beans — your father wanted to tell you himself. But it looks like you two are going to have
a little sister, or a little brother, or — given
how twins run in our family — two little sisters
or brothers."

"Wow!" Stacy said, really surprised.

Alix didn't say anything; she just sat there
looking depressed.

"You okay, pumpkin?" Gram asked, reaching
over and rumpling her long curly hair.

"Do you think they'll take my room away for
the baby?" she said in a very small voice. "Make
me sleep in the living room?"

"Oh, no," Gram assured her, but Alix could
hear a joke coming. "Not the living room."

"Out in the hallway," Stacy joined in.

"I was thinking they'd put her in the elevator," Gram said.

"Well, that'd have its ups and downs," Stacy

said, and reached over and tickled Alix to the ground while Gram laughed until tears were streaming down her cheeks. Jake even forgot his bone and came over to jump on everyone and step into the chocolate cake.

Chapter 4

The next morning, Stacy and Alix woke up within seconds of each other, as they always did when they were together. The already hot summer sun was pouring through the window of their attic loft room. There was a huge roaring buzz coming from outside.

Stacy, full of energy as usual, bounded out of the top bunk and over to the window to see what the commotion was. She turned back to Alix and explained.

"Gram. Queen of the Rider Mowers. Cutting the backyard down to size."

"What time is it? Did we oversleep?"

"Probably," Stacy said, going to look for her watch. "We usually do. We are just not, I'm afraid, ever going to really get ourselves on farm time. I mean, I know there's a rooster here. Ben. I've seen him. And I assume that, being a bona fide rooster, he crows at the crack of dawn, but have you ever heard him?"

Alix shook her head.

"Me, neither," said Stacy, who'd just found her watch under the pile of stuff around the bed. "Ten-thirty. We've got to get a move on. Want to go ride the horses?"

"Oh, yeah!" Alix said, pulling herself sleepily out of bed, rummaging around in her bag for her jeans.

"And this year *you* ride Lightning Bolt, and I'll ride Old Rocking Chair," Stacy said, on her way downstairs. "Give you a challenge."

"Oh, no! Stace!" Alix said, running after her sister, not sure if she was kidding or not. Lightning Bolt was a terror. Old Rocking Chair was a senior citizen among horses. Now he was nearly as tame as the mechanical horse Alix used to ride in front of the supermarket, which was still just her speed.

The twins went to the stables and looked in on Nell and her colt, who was so cute and rickety on his legs they both had to gush over him a little and give him sugar cubes.

"Any ideas for names yet?" Alix said.

Stacy shook her head.

"You?"

"Nope. But I'm working on it."

All morning they rode. Stacy, who *had* just been teasing, took Lightning Bolt and gave Old Rocking Chair to Alix. They took the horses all over Gram's property and into the adjoining state forest, barely getting back in time for lunch with Gram and her farmhand Tully. The girls offered to help them out in the soybean fields, but Gram shooed them away.

"Get yourselves out of here! This is the first day of your vacation. Take the horses over to the quarry this afternoon, why don't you? See if that old swimming hole's up to snuff."

And so they put their towels and suits in a backpack and rode out over the rolling hills to the deep, blue quarry, cool even in the hottest part of the hottest day of summer.

Stacy was the first one in, as usual, taking a high, clean jackknife from the bluff straight down into the water. Alix took the long way in — walking down the winding path leading to the edge of the quarry and lowering herself in slowly, inch by inch.

"It's the healthy way," she said, trying not to look like a wimp. "I read it in a magazine article. It gives your body temperature time to adjust."

"It's the wimpy way," Stacy called back from the water. "It gives your mind a chance to adjust to the fear of getting in. It does not take into account, however, the possibility of an insane splashing maniac twin being in the vicinity."

"No! Don't!" Alix squealed. "You'll be responsible for my body temperature dropping too rapidly. I might get hypothermia and then wouldn't you feel awful?"

But Stacy was merciless. She took an arm and skimmed large sheets of water onto her sister so that Alix was completely soaked before she even got in.

"Rat!" she cried out, but Stacy wouldn't stop until Alix was all the way in.

There was a rope dangling from a tree branch that extended out over the quarry, and the two of them took turns swinging far out over the water on it and letting go and dropping in. They'd been swinging on this old rope since they were both little girls.

Later in the afternoon, the twins brought their journals and went up into the hayloft of Gram's barn.

"Don't you think hay smells sweet, like caramel apples?" Alix said as they climbed the ladder and flopped into the huge pillow of hay.

"You have the craziest sense of smell." Stacy told her. "Remember when you used to love it when Dad pulled into gas stations. You loved the smell of gasoline."

"Still do," Alix said.

"Weird," Stacy said. "But I'll let you read my journal anyway."

They exchanged their looseleaf notebooks, and for a long time lay side by side reading each other's journal pages, getting inside each other's lives — the lives they were now leading separately, miles and worlds apart.

"Sam sounds nice sometimes and a pain other times," Alix observed.

"That about sums it up." Stacy admitted. "Actually, that sort of sums up boyfriends generally."

"I wish I could make sweeping generalizations about boyfriends. I haven't even had *one* yet."

"You will. You just need to find someone who doesn't need to be taken by storm."

"You mean some guy who can stand to wait around for the first three dates where I sit tongue-tied and dying of terminal shyness? What's Sam look like?"

"Oh, he's cute. *Very* cute. Like a surfer."

"Are you in love with him?"

"I don't think so. He's too possessive. And jealous. Being his girlfriend is like being his property. A lot of the guys around school are like that, though. It's hard to get away from. But it keeps me from really caring about him."

"You ever talk with him about this?"

Stacy looked a little surprised and shook her head.

"He'd probably just drop me and start going with Sonia Brown. He's always flirting with her at parties."

"Let me get this straight. He flirts at parties, but he's jealous of you. He treats you like a possession. Next you're going to tell me he makes you pull the ox cart to the marketplace. Stace — haven't you heard about feminism or anything?"

"Yeah, but the guys at Joshua Tree High haven't. Especially the football players. They're kind of like little kings around school. You're supposed to feel lucky just to be going with one of them. I guess you can't expect Matt Dillon sensitivity, too."

"This doesn't sound good," Alix said.

"I know," Stacy admitted. "It gets me down, but I don't know what to do about it. Now, *you* could probably get him into line in about a minute. You'd just give him one of your frosty glares, and that hulk would be cowering under the pool table."

Alix had to smile a little. She liked thinking

of getting this bullying boyfriend of her sister's to behave.

"And you could for sure pass geometry for me. Actually, you could probably live my life much better than I am at the moment."

"Oh, well, you could probably live mine better than I am. Except for playing the violin. But you'd be so charming to Martine that she'd be buying you presents and baking you cakes — well, microwave cakes anyway."

"I can see from your journal that she's a big problem for you. I think maybe you two have just gotten yourselves into a stand-off. She tries to be nice and you reject her because you think she's being phoney, and that makes her not like you so that the next time she's nice to you, it really is kind of phoney. Somebody has to break the cycle."

"Well, like I say, you could probably do it, but not me. You could probably also find me a boyfriend in about a day, I'll bet."

"Yeah," Stacy said, dreamily, lying back into the hay, chewing on a long stalk of it, "we could solve all the problems of each other's lives all right. If only we were in each other's shoes."

Neither of them said anything. They didn't even look at each other. They didn't have to. Each knew exactly what the other was thinking. *They could switch places!* The pause in the conversation hung between them full of all the millions of questions they were asking and answering in their heads. Finally, Stacy turned to Alix and said, "Well?"

"Do you think we could really pull it off?" Alix wondered.

"I don't know," Stacy said, laughing. "Maybe. But . . ."

"But what?"

"But a million things. Your violin for one. How could I ever convince anyone I was you if I even got near it? I wouldn't know which end of the bow to hold."

"No problem. Professor Faraci's going to Italy for the summer. I forgot to tell Dad and Martine. So all you have to do is pretend you're going to the conservatory, and then just stay out for a couple of hours. I almost never practice at home, so they won't notice a thing."

"But won't you get out of practice if you don't play all summer?"

Alix thought a minute.

"I'll stuff my violin in my duffel. We'll just get you a case in town and you take that back to Chicago empty. Just carry it around with you, and I'll have my violin to practice on out in California. I'll manage to find someplace where no one will see me. I wouldn't want to ruin your reputation as a total jock and non-cultural type."

"Wait a minute. You're talking like it's already decided," Stacy said.

"Well, isn't it? We can just do it for the summer. Straighten out each other's messy lives and then, when we get together at Dad's for Labor Day, we'll just change back, and no one'll be the wiser."

"Aren't you forgetting one small detail?"

"What?" Alix said.

"You'd have to cut your hair."

"Oh, no! I can't!" Alix put her hand to her shoulder-length curls. "This mop has taken me three years to grow to perfection."

"Secret agents have to suffer for their profession."

"Oh, boy," Alix said, and then thought one step further, and groaned.

"What?" Stacy asked.

"If I have to get it cut here, that means going to the only haircutting shop in Cordelia."

"Oh, no!" Stacy said, slapping a hand to her forehead. "Zelda's Salon de Beauté!"

Chapter 5

The twins stood on the sidewalk of Cordelia's main street, in front of Zelda's Salon de Beauté. They looked gloomily through the window at the faded posters of hairstyles from bygone eras — a pageboy from the fifties, a fluffy bouffant style from the sixties. There was nothing that looked remotely like a style of today. Zelda had been cutting their grandmother's hair for years — and giving her exactly the same hairdo. It was okay for Gram, who didn't care about high style and just wanted something that wasn't "hard to keep up," but it made Alix nervous. Maybe she *should* have let Stacy cut her hair this morning when Stacy had jokingly snipped a lock from Alix's head and Alix had laughingly shrieked, "Stop!"

Alix had been feeling blue all the way into town, but now, looking at the stark reality of

Zelda's, she sank to the bottom of the pit of despair. "I guess I can always wear a bag over my head for the first couple of months," she said to her sister.

"Maybe it won't be so bad," Stacy said, trying to sound like she believed this. "Maybe Zelda's taken a refresher course since she put up these pictures."

"Right," Alix said sarcastically. "The Zelda Corporation probably flies her up to New York every season to work out with Vidal Sassoon."

"I know it looks bad," Stacy admitted, "but we don't really have any choice. Zelda is the only game in town, except for Bill's Barber Shop, and I don't think you want to risk getting a crew cut."

And so they both took deep breaths, pushed against the front door, and walked into a blast of air conditioning and the smell of permanent wave solution.

"Yes?" Zelda said from the back of the shop, where she was putting tight curlers on a woman's hair. Then she peered more closely at them. "Why as I live and breathe, is that Nora Wyatt's twin granddaughters?"

"Yes," they said simultaneously, then Stacy stepped forward.

"Uh, my sister would like to get her hair cut."

"Well, as you can see . . ." Zelda said, gesturing to the woman in the chair in front of her, "I'm up to my elbows in this here perm at the moment. But I think my daughter Jolene might be able to fit you in." She turned and shouted toward the back of the shop. "Jo-leeeen!"

Within seconds the drape in the doorway was pulled aside and out came the most amazing person the twins had ever seen in Cordelia. She was maybe twenty, and totally New Wave. Her hair was dyed deep black, with a brush of purple on the long bangs. One side was shaved about an inch above her ear, which had three earrings, all skulls and crossbones, dangling from it. She was wearing a black leather mini-skirt and a tiger print halter top. The twins stood watching her with their mouths open. Their fear of Alix getting a haircut that was straight out of 1950 had completely disappeared — replaced by a fear that she was about to get a haircut straight out of the year 2001.

"Jolene, honey, you got time for a cut?" Zelda asked her daughter.

Alix held her breath. Maybe Jolene's schedule would be too full. But no.

"Sure. No problem," Jolene said and then turned to Alix and Stacy and said, "Twins — freaky."

"Oh, not *so* freaky," Stacy said, in case Jolene was getting any ideas about them being punkers.

"So whatcha interested in?" Jolene said as she sat Alix in the chair and wrapped her in a pink plastic cape. "Something sort of mondo bizarro?"

"Oh, not quite mondo," Alix said. "And definitely not bizarro."

Stacy came over and pointed at herself.

"She wants a cut just like mine." She turned around twice so Jolene could get a good look.

"Oh, sure," Jolene said. "I can do that." And then after a long pause, she added, "I think."

Alix crossed her fingers and shut her eyes. Stacy sat down in the bank of waiting chairs and watched as Alix's terrific head of hair became a huge pile of auburn clippings on the floor around the chair. After about twenty minutes of concentrated snipping, Jolene put down her scissors and picked up her blow dryer, and when she was done, she tapped on the top of Alix's head.

"You can come out now," she teased her. "It's all over."

Alix peered into the mirror. It was pretty weird to suddenly have short hair, but she had to admit it didn't look all that bad. And then Stacy got up and came over and stood next to her. They both looked in the mirror and had the same thought.

"Far out," Stacy whispered. "We look exactly alike. No one in the world could tell us apart now."

Alix nodded and said under her breath, "It's going to work. We're really going to pull this off."

Chapter 6

The twins took a long time walking home. They followed the train tracks that ran through town, then cut through the fields and farmland surrounding Cordelia. The late afternoon summer sun was warm on their backs as they ambled slowly along, trying to think of all the things about their separate lives they needed to tell each other before they made "the switch."

"Oh, did I tell you Mom's been taking pottery classes?"

"Pottery?" Alix said amazed.

"Yeah," Stacy said. "She says she's looking for a 'creative outlet.' I personally don't think pots are quite her creative outlet. Everything she makes has the same smooshed sort of look. You'll see. Just remember, if it looks smooshed, it's probably something she made in her class, so don't say anything insulting about it."

"Mom's pottery — smooshy. Got it," Alix said. "Oh. Here's one for you. Martine's kind of a health food person. She buys all these special products that cost about three times what regular grocery store products cost. Like this organic cashew butter. It costs about the same as pure gold. So if you go to make yourself a peanut butter and jelly sandwich, don't use her precious cashew butter or she'll throw a fit."

"I could just say I'm organic, too."

"I already tried that once. She just gave me her multo frosto look and said nobody who eats Little Bob's Choco-Marshmallow Snak Cakes — my favorite treat, I must admit — could possibly be organic. She said my system was already so hopelessly polluted with junk food that it wouldn't recognize an organic product if it came down the tube, and so it was a total waste of the jillion dollars an ounce that organic cashew butter costs for me to eat it."

"Boy," Stacy said and whistled a little. "I guess I won't be touching that old cashew butter. Anything else? No, wait . . . here's one for you. Sam and I go running together every Saturday morning."

"Oh," Alix said.

"Yeah. Four miles."

"Four miles?" Alix screamed. "I can't run four blocks."

"You'll have to work it out."

Alix tried to imagine what she was going to do about this; she couldn't, then got caught by a thought of her own. "Here's something for you to remember," she told Stacy. "I've been going to a series of lectures on the Impressionist painters. Down at the Art Institute."

"I'll have to remember to skip those."

"You can't. Dad and Martine think it's fascinating. They always ask me a ton of questions when I get back."

"Argh. How am I going to sit through . . . how many of these lectures are left?"

"They just started. I think there'll be about eight left when you get back. Look on the schedule in my top desk drawer. Oh, and I have my hidden savings in there, too. Under the drawer liner paper."

"You have savings? That's incredible. I don't have a cent saved. Actually, I'm three weeks ahead of my allowance already, but Mom's pretty good about it. How *much* do you have saved?"

"Stacy. Please. Only in an emergency."

"I promise. Break glass and take out money. Do clothes count as an emergency?"

Alix just glared at her sister.

"Okay. Only in a real, true, dire emergency," Stacy said, and crossed her heart with her first two fingers. "Oh, I'd better tell you all about Rosalie. I'm afraid she's going to be your best friend for the next two months."

"Will I like her?"

"Oh, boy, I don't even know if *I* like her. She's got a good heart, but . . ."

"But what?"

"Well, Joshua Tree's a small town and most people there have never been outside it much. They think, well they're more concerned with what's happening right around them, not so much about what's going on in the whole wide world. Rosalie's kind of like that. She's going with the neatest guy in school and gets pretty good grades, and after high school she's going to go to work for her parents. They own the best restaurant in town — Howe's. She's got it all mapped out. She thinks I should have it all mapped out by now, too. That I should marry Sam and become a phys ed teacher because I'm such a jock. But I don't know if that's my plan. I don't think at fifteen I really *have* to have a plan. But in Joshua Tree . . . well, you'll see."

"Does Martine live in Joshua Tree?" Alix asked.

Stacy laughed and shook her head. "No, of course not."

"Then it's my kind of town. Oh, I shouldn't forget to tell you. Some nights the three of us — me and Dad and Martine — play Perquackey."

"Per*what*?"

"It's this word game. Martine taught us how to play. Don't worry about it. I'm not very good at it, so even if you're terrible, they won't think anything's wrong."

"Boy. Perquackey and painting lectures. Sounds like I'm going to die of excitement," Stacy teased her sister. "You'd really better pass geometry for me."

"No problem."

"And shape up Sam."

"Okay. Boy, it's funny. I could never even think of doing all this stuff for real. But since I'm just going to be impersonating you, it's like a part in some play. I'll just be acting, and that doesn't seem very scary at all. But you've got to do your share in return."

"Like get things smoothed out with Martine."

"*And* find me a boyfriend."

"No problem. Any special requirements?"

Alix sat down on a fallen log by the side of

the tracks and thought about this for a minute. Stacy fell onto the ground next to her, pulled out a long straw of grass and started chewing on it while she listened to her sister's boyfriend specifications.

"Sensitive. And with curly hair. It would be great if he was interested in music — but not required. Oh, and if he was a big reader. . . ."

"I'll try. I'll have to study up on literature and music, though, so I can talk to this guy when I find him. Is there like a book or something that would give me the basics? You know, like one of those condensed notes things?"

Alix looked at her sister to see if she was kidding and when she could see she wasn't, she patted her on the head and said, "Oh, boy. Maybe you'd better just be your charming self. Forget the literature and music conversations."

"I wish I could tell you to forget those four-mile runs," Stacy said, looking up at Alix, "but they're really a big part of my relationship with Sam. The other thing is that I usually beat him."

Gram was in the kitchen fixing dinner when the twins finally got back to the farm.

"Hi, Gram."

"Hi, Gram."

"Hello, girls," Gram said, not turning at first, her attention absorbed by the large pot of potatoes she was mashing. The twins sat down at the table and waited.

"Get yourselves ready for some real country cooking," Gram said as she turned to bring the pot to the table. "We'll put a few pounds on — " She stopped in mid-sentence. Her jaw dropped.

"Well, I'll be. . . ."

"What do you think of my new haircut?" Stacy said, patting the back of her head, testing Gram. If they could fool another twin, they could fool anyone.

"How do I know you're really Alix?" Gram said, not about to fall easily.

"You mean you can't tell for sure?" Stacy teased.

"No one could," Gram admitted. "Your own father couldn't, even when you were babies."

"What do you mean?" Alix asked.

"You two were so alike your mother put name bracelets on you — so's she could tell you apart. Then one day your dad gave you a bath and he forgot the system and just took both bracelets off and washed you both up and then went to put the bracelets back on and had no idea which bracelet went with which twin. So don't go getting smug on me for not knowing which of you is Alix and which one's Stacy. Because the truth is, you don't know either."

They spent the rest of the week briefing each other on every detail they could think of about their lives, but still having all the fun they usually did at Gram's — riding the horses and swimming in the quarry and going around with Gram to flea markets (she bought two more weather vanes), and helping with farm chores like feeding the chickens and milking Gram's three cows and working in the big vegetable garden out back and going into Cordelia for a big dance at the VFW hall.

The dance was for all ages, but turned out to be a lot more fun than they were expecting. They met a couple of guys who were cousins and great dancers, and Alix wasn't at all nervous around them. She was sort of already getting into Stacy Mode and not feeling as shy as she usually did. The weird thing was that Stacy was sort of ill-at-ease, which she *never* was around guys. It was as if she were going into Alix Mode.

The day they were to leave, both twins were

edgy and filled with second thoughts.

"We can just forget the whole thing," Stacy suggested as they bumped around in the back of Gram's truck on their way to the airport and train station.

"No. It's only for two months. We've gone through all our briefings, and I know we can solve the problems in each other's lives. Plus it's just too exciting to resist — the fun of fooling everyone, and the chance to live a whole other life for a while. If we don't do it, we'll always wonder what would have happened if we did."

Stacy nodded. Alix was probably right.

At the train depot in Cordelia, Gram handed Stacy a big brown bag.

"A little foraging food for the train ride back to Chicago, Alix."

Stacy, making her first move as "Alix," peered into the bag.

"Enough lunch for me and three other people," she commented.

"It's my grandmother's chromosome," Gram said. "I can't help myself. I keep your pictures in my wallet and overfeed you and" — here she got a little teary-eyed — "and wish you didn't have to go back home after just two weeks."

Stacy gave Gram a big hug, then turned and gave Alix one.

"Good luck," she whispered in her sister's ear.

"All aboard!" the conductor cried out.

Stacy hopped onto the train just as it was starting to pull away from the depot. She waved at Gram and Alix as she disappeared, along with the train, into the wheat fields.

Gram put an arm around Alix as they walked together back to the truck, to take Alix to St. Louis to catch her plane.

"You girls should have a very interesting summer," she said.

Alix tensed up. Did Gram know? She was, after all, a twin herself, and so more tuned into Stacy and Alix than anyone else.

"Uh . . . just how do you mean *interesting*?" Alix asked, trying to sound casual.

"Oh," Gram said, looking away vaguely, "I just meant that you're fifteen this summer. It's . . . uh . . . a very interesting age. I remember it well myself."

Alix looked over. She thought she saw a glimmer of something in Gram's eyes. An "I know more than you think I know" look. But she couldn't be sure.

"Yes," Gram went on, now talking more to

herself than to Alix. "A *very* interesting summer."

Probably more interesting than any of us can guess, Alix thought, wondering — now that it was just a little too late — if she and Stacy weren't making a big mistake.

Chapter 7

For Alix, the switch was weird from the very start. She got off the plane in the tiny Joshua Tree airport, and there was her mother. She looked great. Alix hadn't seen her since Christmas in Chicago, and felt huge sentimental tears welling up inside her. She was just about to burst out crying when she got hold of herself. In the nick of time, she remembered that she was *supposed* to be Stacy, that she'd only left her mother a couple of weeks ago. She should be happy to see her mother, but not hysterical like those relatives in newspaper stories — reunited after thirty years. And so Alix bit her lower lip, tried for a natural looking smile and gave her mother a casual hug.

"How was it at Gram's?" Karen Wyatt asked her daughter.

"Oh, you know — it's always fun," Alix replied, trying to be vague. So much of what she and Stacy had done at the farm was make plans for the switch, and she couldn't tell her mother about any of that. She tried to think of something she *could* tell.

"And, I . . .uh, I mean *Alix* got her haircut." It was so weird talking about herself like she wasn't there. Everything about this conversation was making her tense.

"How was the little colt?" her mom asked now.

"Oh, he's so cute. Still rickety on his little legs, and with the biggest eyes."

"Did you finally come up with a name for him?"

"Uh, yeah. We called him Little Secret."

Alix's mother gave her a perplexed look. "What an odd name. Why'd you pick *that*?"

"Oh, I don't know," Alix said, looking away, unable to meet her mother's eye. "It just seemed to suit him."

They went out to the parking lot and Alix got in next to her mother. She tried to unclench and ask some casual-sounding question.

"So how are things going at work?" she said in what she hoped was a nonchalant tone, but she could hear her voice cracking a little. By now she felt like she was going to burst from all the confusing feelings rushing around inside her — happiness to see her mother, nervousness that she was going to blow the secret. How was she ever going to pull off a whole summer as Stacy if she couldn't even make it through the ride home from the airport?

"Not so good," her mother said. "They're cutting back, and I had to fire three people in my department."

"Oh, no!" Alix wailed. She'd meant to sound politely concerned, but was so nervous that she completely overreacted and wound up practically screaming. Then on top of it, she couldn't hold her tears back anymore and just let them go.

Karen Wyatt looked over at her daughter in amazement.

"It's okay, honey," she said, reaching over and patting Alix's shoulder. "We're trying to relocate them with a subsidiary company. Boy, I never knew you were so sensitive to my employees' problems."

"It's just so sad," Alix said, trying to get a grip on herself so she wouldn't look like more of a lunatic than she already did.

"How's Alan?" Alix asked quickly, dabbing at her eyes with a tissue from her pocket, trying desperately to find a subject she could talk about without getting totally bent out of shape.

"Oh, he's fine. He left some more records for you. Your special requests, I gather."

"Oh. Great," Alix said, but she was distracted. They were driving through town now and she was looking out the window intently. She wanted to make sure she remembered where things were in Joshua Tree. She'd only been out there once before, a few months after Stacy and their mom had moved out. There was the Burger King, and the library, and the little shopping center with the quad theaters. And there was Joshua Tree High.

Alix slapped her forehead.

"What's the matter?" her mother asked.

"Mosquito," Alix lied. Actually she'd just remembered something terrible. How could she have forgotten to get a diagram or something from Stacy of the high school's layout? How was she going to look like she knew her way around when summer school started next week? And she couldn't call Stacy, not so soon after they'd gotten back. That would just look too fishy. She'd have to figure her way around on her own. She wondered how many other crucial items they'd forgotten to talk about at the farm.

They drove into Rancho Grande Estates and pulled up in the driveway of her mother's town house. When they went into the living room,

Alix was really glad Stacy had warned her about the pottery. What she hadn't mentioned was that there was so much of it. Nearly every horizontal surface was filled with smooshed clay objects painted with bright abstract designs. They were all really terrible. If she hadn't known ahead of time that they were made by her mother, she would've burst out laughing.

"Your requests," her mother said, handing her a stack of record albums. "From Alan. Try not to wear them — and me — out, playing them every minute of the day."

Alix looked through the selection. The Pogues. Talking Heads. Suzanne Vega. She didn't recognize any of them. She'd have to try to play them once in a while though, to keep up the appearance of being Stacy. She could always put earplugs in while the records were on. Basically she hated rock. When she played music for herself, it was strictly classical all the way. Well, not for the next couple of months it wouldn't be. For the next couple of months she was going to be Stacy and Stacy would *never* listen to classical. She didn't know Beethoven from Bach. And if Alix was going to pull this off, she had to not only look and sound like her sister, she had to act like her, too. In every single way. Down to the tiniest detail.

"You've got some messages," her mother was saying now. "Rosalie called yesterday. She had the day you were coming back wrong. And Sam left about a ten-minute message on the tape this morning. You can play it back. Something complicated. He has to do something for his dad tonight and so you're supposed to meet him at Bill's. There's a party."

She had no idea who Bill was or where he lived. There was no way she'd ever be able to find this party. She was in dire need of an excuse to not have to go to it.

"Oh, you probably don't want me going out, it being my first night back and all," she tried.

"No, it's okay," her mother said. "You start summer school next week. This is really your only summer vacation, so you should just enjoy yourself."

"Argh," Alix said under her breath as she took her suitcase and headed down the hall toward Stacy's bedroom. She pushed open the door and her "argh" turned into "eek!" Alix was a neatness freak. Back in her room in Chicago, the books on her shelves were arranged alphabetically, by author. Her records, by composer. Her underwear was folded into squares and stacked neatly in the top drawer of her dresser. Her socks were rolled up, arranged by color in the second drawer. How could she have forgotten that her sister was the World's Biggest Slob, a charter member of Slobs Anonymous? The room she was staring at now looked like it had been bombed. Clothes were strewn everywhere. Magazines, record jackets, half-finished cans of soda, a plate with three cookies — each with a bite out of it.

"Not a pretty picture," her mother said, suddenly standing behind her. "I had a brief temptation to clean it, but I resisted."

"I guess it does need a little straightening up," Alix said, already rolling up her sleeves, ready to dive in and do everything short of steaming off the old wallpaper. But then the phone rang. Somewhere. From under something. They both groped around as it rang and rang. Finally, from under a pile of running clothes, Alix's mother pulled a receiver.

"It's for you," she said, handing it to Stacy. "Mr. Right."

"How's my girl?" a male voice said on the other end of the line.

"Hi, Sam," Alix said, knowing that's who it had to be.

"Happy to be back?"

"Well, I just got here. . . ."

"I mean are you happy to know you're going to be seeing your boyfriend tonight?"

"Uh, oh, yeah. Sure. At the party. Your message got kind of garbled on the tape. I'm supposed to meet you, but I can't make out the address."

"What address?" he said. "It's just at Bill's. What do you want — an engraved invitation? Be there around eight, okay?"

"I, uh . . ."

"Oh, here comes my dad. I'm going with him to pick up our air conditioner from the shop. See you tonight."

"Yeah, okay," Alix said, hanging up. She had no idea how she'd find Bill's house. But what else could she have said? That she'd fallen from a horse at the farm and had temporary amnesia? Too farfetched. Besides, her mom had been standing right there. No, she'd just have to figure out how to get to Bill's. Somehow.

"I guess I'll call Rosalie back," she told her mother, who nodded and left the room.

Alix got out the little notebook of briefing stuff Stacy had made for her and found Rosalie's number and punched it out on the phone. An unfamiliar girl's voice answered.

"Rosalie? It's Al . . .Stacy."

"I *know* who it is, silly. I haven't forgotten your voice in two weeks. Did you have a fabulous time?"

"Fabulous. Listen, are you going to the party at Bill's tonight?"

"Of course."

"Well, would you mind picking me up?"

"Funny girl. Always making jokes. Or did you break a leg and can't walk one block?"

"I . . . uh . . ."

"Oh, and don't forget to bring your swim suit. Bill's folks got a pool put in their backyard."

"Oh, right. Well, see you there."

She sat on Stacy's bed and heaved a small sigh of relief. If Bill's house was only a block from hers, and there was a pool, she ought to be able to find it with a little walking. And if she waited until after eight there ought to be lights and party sounds. She was beginning to feel like a pretty swift detective. Maybe this wasn't going to be so hard after all. Situations would come up, but she'd just be fast and foxy and find a way out of them. No problem.

Just then, her mother came into the room and sat down on the rumpled bed next to her offering a bowl of something green and another bowl of taco chips.

"What's this?" Alix said.

"What's this, she asks," her mother mocked her. "Only your absolute favorite snack in the whole world — guacamole with extra jalapeño peppers!"

Oh, boy, Alix thought as she took a chip and

dipped it in the avocado. She'd forgotten that Stacy was a maniac for hot foods. To Alix, ginger ale was a little too spicy. As she sat looking with dread at the chip, she wondered how she could have ever thought she and Stacy were exactly alike. It was rapidly becoming clear how *incredibly* different they were!

Chapter 8

Stacy got down off the train and instantly heard someone squeal, "Alix! You cut your hair!" Martine. She was there on the platform with Stacy's dad.

"Yeah," Stacy said, reaching around and patting her hair like it was a tremendously new style when it actually looked exactly the same as it had for years. "Like it?"

"Oh, yes!" Martine said enthusiastically. "So much perkier than that dreadful rag mop you had!"

Stacy could see why Martine and Alix clashed. Alix was so reserved. Martine was so bubbly. Not to mention that Martine was kind of a social klutz. The couple of times Stacy had met her, she'd said things like this, insulting you when she meant to pay a compliment. She'd probably done this a few too many times to

Alix and wound up hurting her feelings. Stacy felt above all this pettiness, though — in a perfect position to sort out the problems between her sister and their stepmother.

"Aw, she looks cute any way you look at her," Stacy's dad said, giving her a hug and taking her suitcase. She was really happy to see him. He looked great. Very happy. Clearly life with Martine suited him. If she looked on the bright side, she could get used to seeing Martine and the baby and maybe even Alan Sakamoto as additions to their expanding happy family. Stacy always tried to look on the bright side. Usually she succeeded. Except with geometry.

All the way back to the apartment, Stacy concentrated on getting into Alix's mindset — Alix Mode — thinking like her sister, perceiving things the way *she* would. She figured this was going to be her key to successfully impersonating Alix. The way method actors get *inside* the characters they play.

As a first step, she tried to enjoy a few moments of solitude in Alix's bedroom. She looked around and said to herself, I *enjoy* the neurotic neatness in here. Really I do. I'm going to lie down on this perfectly made bed and not rumple it up. I'm going to turn on the boom box here and enjoy this classical music even though it makes me crazy.

Stacy was only able to do this for five minutes before she leapt out of bed, shut off the music, undressed, put running shorts and a T-shirt on, then put her clothes on over them, stuffed her running shoes in Alix's violin case and headed out of the apartment. Alix Mode or no Alix Mode, Stacy was going to go nuts if she couldn't get out and run.

"Going somewhere?" Martine said. Stacy had to admit Martine did have a sickeningly sweet way of talking.

"Just down to the conservatory for an hour or so."

"Well, don't be late," Martine said, wagging a finger at Stacy. "We're all going out to dinner someplace special tonight. Steve, uh . . . your father and I have a little announcement to make."

I wonder what that might be? Stacy said to herself. To Martine, she just said, "Okay" in a flat, dull voice. In the hallway, waiting for the elevator, it struck her. Maybe this was the same voice Alix had told her she used with Martine — "Alix the Undead." Maybe she really *was* getting into Alix Mode.

As soon as she got into the park, Stacy stopped along the running trail, peeled her top layer of clothes, getting down to her running

74

gear, stuffed the clothes and shoes into the violin case and hid the case deep inside a big bush. She did a few stretching exercises and headed out for a brisk run. She knew this strip of the lakefront like the back of her hand. Before she'd moved to California, this was her old running path. And before that it was her bike path, before that her tricycle path — the stomping ground of her childhood. Being back here, with the spectacular blue lake on one side of her, the brilliant green park on the other, she felt overwhelmed with nostalgia.

In Joshua Tree, there weren't that many runners. Mornings, she usually ran with a couple of kids from Rancho Grande Estates, and then on Saturdays with Sam. Often they didn't see any other runners the whole time they were out. But here in Chicago, it was like a freeway of runners and joggers and brisk walkers and even a few people just ambling along through the middle of it, enjoying the late summer afternoon. She just loved the rush of people in the big city. It was one of the things she really missed now that she was living in a small town. And at this particular instant, she was really happy she and Alix had made the switch. And she felt sure it was going to work out great.

Stacy got up to her pace and ran two miles toward downtown — "The Loop" — then headed back north toward home. When she finished, she was in the park in front of the apartment building where her dad and Martine lived. She was catching her breath, bending over doing some toe-touches, oblivious to what was going on around her. But then, when she stood up, her attention was instantly snagged by a skinny guy, about her age, maybe a little older. Curly black hair and little horn-rim glasses. He was wearing the oldest, baggiest pair of bermudas she'd ever seen, and an equally beat-up polo shirt. Definitely not cute in any standard way — not like Sam — but still, there was something about him that made her curious to know more about him. Maybe it was that he was training a dog he kept calling "Spot," which was absolutely plain white with not a spot on it.

"Sit, Spot," the guy was saying. Not only did this dog not have any spots, but it wasn't anywhere close to sitting, either. It was standing, tail wagging happily, looking up at the guy without the vaguest idea what he was supposed to be doing.

"Sit, Spot," the guy tried again. Stacy had to laugh at the dog's name. And at the total lack of success this guy was having. He heard and looked up at her.

"Ah, I see you are a professional dog trainer.

That must be why you're laughing at me. You yourself could get this dog to sit in a second, I'm sure."

Stacy threw up her hands in protest.

"Not me. I probably couldn't get him to munch a bone. And actually, I was only partly laughing at what a terrible job you're doing. The other part I was laughing at was his name."

"Oh. Well, it makes sense if you know him. He definitely has a Spot personality."

"You mean *dog*-ality," Stacy corrected.

The guy smiled.

"I only got him a week ago. At Anti-Cruelty. He'd been brought back twice. He's a little nutty is why, I guess. But so am I, so it seems to be working out. Sitting's only the beginning for him. After he's got this knocked, I'm moving him up to 'rolling over' and 'playing dead.' Then playing poker. Not too many dogs can play a good game of poker, you know. They start grinning when they get a good hand."

Stacy had to laugh.

"My grandmother's got a dog that smiles," she said.

"All dogs smile," he said. "You just have to know the kind of jokes they like. Hey, my name's Brendan Miller."

"St . . . I mean Alix. Alix Wyatt. You live around here?"

Brendan nodded, then pointed at a high-rise building a few up from Stacy's.

"I've seen you around," he said. "Not running, though. Don't you play the violin or something? You carry one of those serious little cases?"

"Oh, yeah. Sometimes. Not this summer, though." She tried to think fast. "I . . . uh . . . sprained my wrist in this big concert and they want me to rest it up for a couple of months."

"Oh. Too bad. I would've liked to hear you play. Maybe we could go to a concert sometime, though. I really like classical music. Almost as much as I like jazz."

"What about rock?"

"Some of it," he said. Spot barked.

"*He* loves it," Brendan said.

"A very cool dog, I must say," Stacy said. "What about movies? Do you like those?"

"Oh, yeah," Brendan said. "Especially old ones."

"Me, too," Stacy said.

"Then you must go to the Music Box," he said.

"The what?"

"How can you love old movies and not know about the Music Box?" he said, really amazed.

"Well, uh . . . I've been sort of spending my time . . ."

"Practicing, I know," he said, finishing her sentence for her. "You musicians. But you have to take a break sometimes, and now with your wrist sprained, you should have plenty of free time. Why don't you meet me here tomorrow and I'll bring the Music Box schedule. They change their bill every day, so you can see a huge amount of great old pictures. You can look and see what you're interested in and if I'm interested, too, maybe I'll let you bring me along with you."

"Oh, you will, will you?" she said, putting her hands on her hips in mock indignation. Then she looked at the sun behind the high rise buildings and said quickly, "What time is it, do you know?"

Brendan looked at his watch.

"Six-thirty."

"Oh, boy. Got to run. My dad and stepmother are taking me out to dinner."

"Oh. Okay. See you tomorrow, then. Spot says good-bye, too."

They both looked over at the dog who, now that he wasn't being trained, was sitting perfectly. Stacy and Brendan both cracked up, and Stacy ran off, waving as she went.

As soon as she'd rounded a tree-lined bend, she hid behind one of the trees and waited and watched until Brendan and Spot had wandered off. Then she went back, fetched the violin case out of the bushes and put her jeans and shirt on over her now-sweaty running outfit.

"How pleasant," she said to herself sarcastically. She couldn't do this every time she wanted to go running. No way. "I'm afraid," she said under her breath as she headed toward home, "*Alix* is just going to have to become a little more of a jock."

"Wow," Stacy said in a rush of breath as she and her father and Martine entered the restaurant. It was the fanciest place anyone had ever taken her to. Dark wood paneling on the walls and white-white tablecloths and good-looking waiters in black pants and tux shirts rushing around.

"The cuisine here is *international*," Martine said as the three of them were opening their menus. Stacy could see that Martine could get a little irritating with the way she acted like she was showing you the world. Like she was the World Hostess. It would make anyone want to be sarcastic. Like right now, Stacy wanted to say, "Yeah, we eat international cuisine all the time — at the *International* House of Pancakes."

But of course she couldn't. She had to act like she was Alix and happy to be here in this swanky place, about to eat international cuisine and be told that Martine was going to have a baby. Stacy focused on her mission: turning things around, getting Alix and Martine back on better footing.

"Everything looks delicious, Martine," she said. "Maybe you could pick for me." She hoped this didn't sound completely phoney.

"Why, I'd be delighted," Martine said, and smiled across the table. She scanned the large menu and then, when the waiter had come up and was standing ready for their order, she said, "For starters, I'll have the paté. And Alix will have the escargots."

When the waiter had nodded and disappeared, Stacy asked Martine, "Just what was that you ordered for me? It sure sounded international."

"Snails," Martine said sweetly. There was no way to know if she was being deliberately awful, or just being totally oblivious to what a fifteen-year-old girl might want to eat.

"You're kidding," Stacy said, hopefully.

"Of course not. Trust me. You'll love them.

Now listen, darling, because your daddy and I want to tell you our little secret." She reached for Steve Wyatt's hand and held it across the table. Stacy put her eager look on her face and waited.

"You're going to have a little brother or sister," she beamed. "We're going to have a baby!"

Stacy was prepared. She went into her method acting impression of an ecstatic person.

"Oh, Martine! That's wonderful! Oh, I hope you'll let me baby-sit!" Maybe this was going too far.

But no, Martine took it as a sincere offer.

"You're so sweet!" she said, then turned to Steve. "Isn't she, honey?"

Stacy thought she saw a glint of suspicion in her father's eye. She remembered that as "Alix," she probably shouldn't be quite *this* sweet. She thought for a second, then added, "Of course I charge double the usual rate for family members."

She saw her dad relax at the joke and Martine laughed, too. This was going to be a breeze. She'd fix things right up for old Alix. Martine wasn't so bad. Stacy held on to this opinion until the cute waiter set a plate down in front of her. On it were six poor little dead snails peeking out of their shells.

"Sorry, folks," she said to Martine and her dad and the waiter as she got up from the table and headed for the ladies room. "I think I'm going to have to check out for a minute."

Later that night, lying in bed, playing Alix's radio low on a rock station, Stacy started off thinking about Martine and the snails and the cheeseburger the restaurant had come up with to replace them. But then this whole scene disappeared from her mind, and in its place there was a skinny guy in baggy bermudas. Stacy was puzzled by her interest in Brendan. Not her usual type at all. Then it dawned on her. He was *exactly* her sister's type. She really *was* going into Alix Mode. She was finding the guy her sister would have found, if only Alix weren't so shy.

She rolled over and looked at the read-out on the digital clock by the side of the bed. Ten-thirty. That would make it eight-thirty in Joshua Tree. She wondered how Alix was doing on her first night as Stacy. Probably having a great time.

Chapter 9

Alix was beginning to panic. She'd covered every block of houses in every direction from hers. Then she'd gone to the next block over. Anytime she saw a house that looked lit up enough to be holding a party, she went around back to see if there was a pool. So far she hadn't found any pools, but had nearly been bitten by two dogs, banged her head on a tree branch she didn't see in the dark, and accidentally tromped right through somebody's vegetable garden.

She was beginning to panic. She sat down on a curb and tried to think constructively. Rosalie had said the party was only a block away, but by now Alix had gone two and sometimes three blocks over and still could find no sign of this Bill's house. And now she was at the edge of the subdivision, almost at the highway. There wasn't really any further to go. What was she going to do? She just wanted to go back home and fall into bed, but she knew she had to show up for the party, or everyone would be suspicious.

She sat still and thought about what to do next. And gradually, sounds began filtering into her tumble of thoughts. Music. Girls laughing. Boys shouting. Water splashing. *Splashing?* She leaped to her feet and started half-walking, half-running in the direction of the sounds. Behind a darkened house, into the backyard and suddenly — there it was! The party! Over in the next backyard, maybe fifty kids were dancing on the patio and jumping and pushing each other into the pool.

Alix flushed with relief and then almost immediately clenched with a new wave of nervousness. How was she going to meet all these "friends" of hers, whom she was supposed to know a million things about, with whom she was supposed to have a million private jokes? She realized in a flash that no amount of briefing she and Stacy could have done would prepare her for this.

But still. She'd come this far. She had to go through with it.

Just try to look normal, she told herself.

Smile. Act relaxed. She hopped the low fence between the yards and came into the party.

"Hey, look who's here!" one of the kids shouted out from the pool.

"Finally," said someone else — a big, beefy red-faced guy with hair the color of straw.

Alix smiled and waved and looked around. A girl with black curly hair came up and said in a low voice, "Remind me to tell you something when no one's around. I heard such a story about Molly . . . uh oh, here comes your b.f."

This must be Rosalie. She matched Stacy's description to a "t." But where was this b.f. — boyfriend? Alix looked around, trying to spot Sam among the guys at the party. She was kind of excited, full of nervousness, but anticipation, too. Before she could find him, though, the beefy guy with the straw-colored hair came over and put his arm around her.

"Sure took your time getting here," he chided her. She smiled and tried to be polite. Who was this jerk? And where was Sam?

"Aren't you going to kiss me hello?" the jerk said now.

Outrageous! Alix thought. The nerve of this guy! And what would Sam say if he overheard this?

She pretended she hadn't heard this guy. He looked pretty peeved and like he was about to say something to her, but then two girls came into the yard and waved.

"Hey, Stacy!" one of them shouted at her.

"Hi, Sam!" the other said as they came up to talk.

And suddenly, sickeningly, it dawned on Alix. This creep was Sam! She thought back on the words Stacy had used to describe him. "Surfer." "Hunk." More like "hulk," she thought. She stood back and looked at him in amazement. This was clearly a case of beauty being in the eye of the beholder. Or a case of two girls going for completely different kinds of guys — even when the girls were twins who thought alike on so many other things.

She tried to look normal and smile and let Sam put his arm around her while he talked with the two girls who'd come up. Because the fact was that even though he was the last guy at the party (maybe the last guy on earth) she would have picked, for the next two months she was going to have to at least pretend to be his girlfriend. Ugh!

The two other girls drifted off, leaving Alix alone with Sam.

"So, I guess the party managed to start without me," she said, trying to make conversation.

Then, explaining why she was an hour and a half late, she added, "I had to help my Mom with something. Last minute."

"What?" he asked.

"Uh . . . we took the car in for an oil change."

"She couldn't do that herself?"

"She likes my company," Alix said.

"Yeah, well so do I," Sam said. "Want to dance or something?" he said, nodding toward the patio.

What a suave guy, she thought sarcastically, and the sarcasm came out in her voice when she replied.

"How could any girl resist such a charming invitation."

He looked at her through narrowed eyes.

"What do you want — I should bow and ask the honor of your presence on the dance floor?" He snapped his fingers and looked down at his faded jeans. "And darn, I forgot to wear my white tie and tails tonight, too."

This was going to be a *great* summer, Alix thought dismally as she walked out onto the patio and began dancing with Sam, mostly as a way to avoid having to *talk* with him.

Sam hardly ever left her side all night. Either they were dancing together, or swimming together, or talking to other kids together. These other kids were pretty nice. She didn't really have a crowd of her own like this back in Chicago. Most of the kids at the conservatory were other musicians and a lot of what they talked about was music — not gossip and TV shows and sports like this.

Talking to Stacy's friends was easy and fun. And it made her feel more regular, and more social, just being able to do it. Of course *how* she did it was by pretending to herself that she was Stacy, Miss Outgoing. While she was impersonating Stacy, Alix didn't have to worry about her usual shyness. She didn't even worry about how she looked in her swimsuit the way she usually did. She just splashed around and enjoyed herself. It was really liberating, as though she was being let out of all the heavy ropes she usually went around in — tongue-tied and bashful and always worrying that whatever she was thinking of saying was going to be the wrong thing and so not saying it. Tonight she said whatever she felt like and everybody laughed when she was trying to be funny and acted interested when she was being serious. It was terrific.

The only bad part was Sam, who was *always there*. Once she managed to get away, to go into the kitchen and get some chips. She ran into Rosalie, who launched breathlessly into a long, non-stop story about somebody named

Molly whose father was a minister and didn't approve of her modeling, but she'd gotten an assignment to do a commercial in Los Angeles and now it was going to be on TV and for sure her father the minister would see it and was she ever going to be in trouble. Plus she was going to have to explain that she'd spent all the money she'd made on clothes instead of putting it toward something responsible like her college tuition.

Alix had no idea who Molly was (she was building a list of about a million questions to ask Stacy when she talked to her), and the story had so many twists and turns she could hardly follow it, but still, talking to Rosalie at least let her out of Sam's clutches for a while. She felt like her shoulder had a permanent dent in it from the weight of his arm all evening.

She was just thinking this when the weight descended again. The Arm. She didn't even have to look over to see who it was.

"Where've you been?" he said, as if she'd gone a thousand miles away and disappeared for ten years. How did Stacy stand this? And why was Sam so possessive? And was there any way to break him out of this without breaking up the relationship? She'd have to do something. Stacy or no Stacy, there was simply no way Alix could spend two months with this guy's arm weighing her down like a stone slab.

At eleven or so, he leaned in and said in a low voice near her ear, "So you want to check out of this party, or what?"

"Oh. Okay," she said, although she was having fun at the moment talking with some of the other kids. But she thought she should at least try to be a decent girlfriend.

They walked around to the front of the house and down the street a ways.

"Hey," he said. "You going to walk right past my car?"

"Oh, sorry," she said. "I was just spacing."

"The girl's with the man of her dreams and she's spacing out," Sam said to the side, as if there was some audience sitting in the bushes.

"Not exactly spacing," Alix said. "I was kind of thinking about you." This was a total lie, but Sam believed it. A big smile came over his face, and he put his arm around her again.

"What were you thinking about me?" he said. "Good thoughts?"

"Uh, well," she said, trying to think of something good she could be thinking about this lunkhead. "Oh, yeah. I was thinking how much I'm going to miss you when you go on the Wilderness Trek next week."

"You will? Well, isn't that sweet," he said and then suddenly, way too fast for Alix to stop it, he had turned around and pulled her toward him and was giving her a big kiss. A big, terrible kiss. Although Alix had never in her fifteen years been kissed by a boy, she still knew that if you felt like your lips were being run through a trash compactor, it was a terrible kiss.

Later, when she was back at her mother's and lying in Stacy's bed, she stayed awake for quite a while thinking about what to do. One possibility was just suffering through the next couple of months with Sam. But that was hard to imagine. Another possibility was breaking up with him and leaving it to Stacy to get back together with him in the fall. But that wouldn't be fair to her sister. And then a third possibility dawned on her. She would work on him. So he wasn't the guy of her dreams. So he *was* the guy of her nightmares. She didn't have to let that get her completely down. She could change him. Make him at least a better Sam. And if she succeeded, Stacy would come home to a much nicer boyfriend. And one who kissed nicely.

"Plan Sam goes into operation tomorrow," she said quietly into the dark bedroom.

Chapter 10

Stacy woke up the next morning in a sweat. She'd been having a terrible nightmare. She was being chased off the edge of a high diving board by a swarm of angry snails. Then falling, falling, falling, into a pool of garlic butter.

"Oh, boy," she said to herself, sitting up in bed, wiping her forehead with the sleeve of her T-shirt. "That Martine and her stupid snails!"

Whenever she woke up weirded out like this, she went for a long run — to clear the dream-webs out of her head. As she pulled on a pair of shorts and tied the laces on her thick-soled running shoes, she hoped her dad and Martine were still sleeping, so she could just slip out of the apartment and into the park.

But as soon as she came out of her room, she could smell something cooking in the kitchen. Something awful. Boiled tire, maybe.

In the kitchen, she found her dad sitting at the table reading a section of the fat Sunday paper while Martine stood in front of the microwave waiting for it to ping.

"Ping."

Martine opened the door and pulled out the bowl of boiled tire. Then, looking up and seeing Stacy standing in the doorway, said, "Oh, 'morning Alix. Want some microwave groats with blackstrap molasses?"

"Uh . . ."

"It's very good for you."

"Yeah. It smells like something that's 'good for you.' I think I'll just make myself a peanut butter and jelly sandwich," Stacy said, opening the jar on the counter.

"Excuse me, young lady," Martine said, "but as you well know, that is not peanut butter. That is my hideously expensive organic cashew butter."

Stacy slapped her hand to her forehead. How could she have forgotten about Martine's stupid cashew butter?

"Uh-oh. Sorry, Martine," she said quickly. "I'm not quite awake yet, I guess. I meant to get" — she foraged around in the cupboards — "this!" She held up the jar. "This corrupt commercial product here — Peanuts 'n Preservatives. Mmmm."

"What are those?!" Stacy's father suddenly interjected, peering over the frames of his glasses, which he'd pushed down on his nose.

"What are what?" Stacy said.

"Those large, white objects on your feet," he said, pointing.

"Oh," Stacy said, trying to sound casual. "Just an old pair of running shoes Stacy gave me in Missouri. I kind of got into running with her down there."

"*You?*" Martine squealed in shock. "Running?"

Stacy had to admit her sister had a point about Martine. There *were* an awful lot of moments when you wanted to press some magic "mute" button so that her lips would still move, but no sound would come out. But Stacy exercised extreme patience and just said, "Yeah, well, I guess it must've been all that fresh country air or something. Anyway, I thought I'd try it here. Just around the block or something."

"Don't you think that might be a little rash?" Martine said, a look of sincere concern spreading over her face. "I mean, someone as droopy and out of shape as you . . . well, maybe you ought to start with a brisk walk. You know, like those exercise programs for the elderly."

Brisk walking? Droopy? Elderly? Stacy was

beginning to see how Martine could get to you — *if* you let her. Which she wasn't going to. She was here on a mission, not to take things personally. Martine made this difficult, though. She said more insulting things without even trying than anyone Stacy had ever known. It was amazing that her job was being a flight attendant, where she had to deal with hundreds of new people every day. Stacy figured — given her average number of insults and foot-in-her-mouth remarks — Martine must wind up insulting about half the passengers on any given flight. This led her into a little flash-fantasy of Martine finally going too far and all the passengers on a plane getting up from their seats, storming down the aisle and tossing Martine out an emergency exit. It was amazing how, even at fifteen, so many of Stacy's fantasies were sort of cartoons. Like the morning before her geometry final, she'd imagined that someone had poured disappearing cream over the school making the whole building vanish. No one could find it and so no one could take their exams. These fantasies were a little childish, she knew, but enormously satisfying.

In real life, though, Stacy responded politely to Martine's unwanted advice, saying, "Thanks. I'll take it slow. I'll just walk around the block, briskly but not *too* briskly."

Of course, just to spite Martine, Stacy ran much faster and a lot farther than she usually did.

Three miles down and then three back up the lakefront, Stacy was panting, bent over one of the park's old stone drinking fountains — splashing water over her face and neck. Trying to cool down. Then she stood up and ran her wet hands through her hair, plastering it back off her face. At this most glamorous moment, she heard someone behind her.

"Alix?"

Stacy turned. It was Brendan, with Spot, who ran over and jumped up on Stacy, wagging his tail like mad.

"Hi, guy," she said, rubbing the dog's neck. "And hi, guy, to you, too," she added to Brendan.

"Spot always gets the girls first," he said. "Of course, his approach is more direct. I can't really jump up on them and wag my tail . . ."

". . . and drool on their hand," Stacy said, showing him hers.

"Exactly. Say, I have the Music Box schedule," he said, pulling it out of the pocket of his Hawaiian-print baggies, which he was wearing with a camouflage T-shirt. Brendan was either a fashion individualist, or a total nerd.

Stacy looked over the schedule.

"Boy, it's great. Look, right here — tonight — they're showing *All About Eve* — one of my all-time favorites!"

"I've never seen it," Brendan said.

"And you call yourself a movie lover?" Stacy teased him. "It's great."

"You want to go?" he asked. "The first show's at seven-ten. I could come by for you."

She looked at him and tried to imagine how Martine and her father would react (a) to someone as unusual-looking as Brendan and (b) to Alix suddenly having a date.

In an instant she saw an entire situation comedy full of stupid jokes and awkward moments and Martine putting her foot in her mouth and poor Brendan being scared off into the night. Here she'd found a prime boyfriend candidate for Alix, and she wasn't about to lose him. Nope, she'd just have to keep him under wraps for a while.

"Uh . . ." she said, ". . . why don't we just meet in front of the show instead? I'm going to be out to dinner with my dad and stepmother and it'd be easier if I just came up from there."

"Okay. Seven, then. By the box office." He gave a little flipping salute and ran off through the park, Spot running on ahead of him.

* * *

After dinner — not out at a restaurant, but a deep-dish, Chicago-style pizza they ordered in — Stacy went to her room and tried to change into a better outfit, but nothing that would seem too much better. She didn't want to attract any attention. She put on the lightest possible amount of blush and just a woosh of mascara so Martine wouldn't notice. And then she took Alix's violin case out of the closet and headed toward the door of the apartment.

"Going to the conservatory," she said as casually as could be.

"Pretty dressed up, aren't we?" Martine said. "And makeup, too."

"Yeah, well, Professor Faraci is having another violin teacher in tonight to hear me play."

"Must mean you're doing all right," Stacy's dad said from in front of the TV, where he was watching a Cubs game. "Maybe you won't wind up playing fiddle in the subway station after all."

Stacy loved her dad's sense of humor. She'd been realizing, these past few days here in Chicago, how much she missed him. Apparently he had a running joke with Alix about her violin playing — lots of job suggestions if she didn't make it into a major orchestra as she hoped. Yesterday, he'd told Stacy she could always play at country hoedowns. Or for those companies who make the music they play in elevators.

"Ha. Ha. Ha," Stacy said, and stuck her tongue out at him.

"Well, have fun," he shouted as she headed for the door, and then after she'd closed it and was already at the elevators, her mind on Brendan, she vaguely heard him add, "I think Martine and I might take in a movie."

Brendan was nowhere to be seen when she got to the theater. She stood in front of its 1920s facade and waited around watching people line up. People who lived in the city had — and she'd noticed this before — a whole different look about them, different from people in Joshua Tree. They looked a little more nervous and intense. In Joshua Tree, people were more relaxed and laid-back. People in Chicago were a little more stylish, too, she thought.

Just as she was having this thought, up walked the least stylish person on earth — although he might well be the most stylish person on *his* planet. Brendan. Tonight he was "dressed-up," which meant he had on a sports jacket. But what a sports jacket! She couldn't be absolutely sure, but she was pretty sure if you put it in an absolutely dark room, the jacket would glow. It was green . . . no, when he moved there was also an orangy color to it. It had lapels that were at least four inches wide and piped in white. To compliment this, he was wearing a wide tie with a picture on it of a man catching a large, leaping fish.

Stacy tried to look as though he were dressed like a normal person.

"Well?" he said, twirling around. "Like it?"

"What can I say?" Stacy said. It was the only noncommittal thing she could come up with.

"I figured that as long as I was having a big date tonight, I'd better find myself a terrific outfit. Had to go to four resale shops before I found this. But now I'm thinking, maybe it's too subtle."

He looked at her questioningly, and they both cracked up.

"Are you always this crazy?" she asked.

"Oh, no," he said. "I'm usually much crazier. You should see me when I'm revved on sugar and caffeine. So come on. Let's go on in and get Cokes and candy bars and see the show."

As they were walking in together, he said, "Why'd you bring your violin? You going to play during the sad parts?"

"Uh, well . . . I just came from a lesson."

"I thought you were going out to dinner."

"Well, *before* that I had a lesson."

"I thought you couldn't play . . . on account of your wrist."

"Well, that's right. But they want me to build it up gradually. First I'm supposed to practice holding the bow for a while." She couldn't believe the string of lies she was telling. Pretty smoothly, though. At least that's what she thought until he looked deep into her eyes and said, "Alix. The way you're always dancing around in a tangle of lies, I get the feeling you've got some big secret. Why don't you just tell me the truth?"

Stacy was stunned. She didn't know what to say.

"I can't," was what she finally told him. "I just can't. Can you accept that? I mean, can we still be friends even if I can't tell you everything about me?"

He thought a few seconds, then nodded. "Okay. For now, anyway."

They were standing under the marquee now and Stacy looked up.

"Oh, look. It's a double bill tonight. After this, they're showing *Double Indemnity*. That's one of my dad's favorites."

"You want to stay for it?" he asked.

"No, I'd better get home after this one. Don't

want to freak out the parental units."

By now they'd moved to the head of the line and he quickly bought them two tickets.

"Hey," she said. "If you're going to pay our way in, I insist on buying the goodies. I'm pretty feminist. It's strictly Dutch Treat with me."

"I don't know how feminist that makes you," he said, standing behind her at the candy counter. "It might just make you Dutch."

This wasn't that funny, she knew. But something about the way he said it. . . . She'd just never met such an odd, funny boy as Brendan. For sure, he wasn't like any of the guys at Joshua Tree High. He was going to be absolutely perfect for Alix. Which was why she couldn't tell him anything about the switch. She had to catch him for Alix, then turn him over to her at the end of the summer without Brendan knowing. This was going to be some trick to pull off.

The movie was great. He loved it as much as she did, especially the part where Bette Davis tells all the people at her party, "Fasten your seat belts. It's going to be a bumpy night."

They were laughing as they came out into the lobby. Stacy noticed they were getting quite a few stares — because of Brendan's jacket — from the people on the other side of the velvet rope, the people waiting for the next movie, *Double Indemnity*.

And then when she saw who two of those people were, she just about kicked herself for not connecting the dots. *Double Indemnity* was her father's favorite movie. *Now* she could vaguely hear him saying as she left that he and Martine might be going out to a show. How could she not have put these pieces together? But she hadn't. And so now here she was, being pushed by the crowd behind them, right up to her dad and Martine, who were already looking at them, attracted by the amazing sight of Brendan's jacket.

"Alix?" her father said.

"Aaaall-ix!" Martine said, about three times louder.

What incredibly humongous lie could she come up with to cover this situation? Brendan was the visiting violin teacher and he'd wanted to hear the strings on the soundtrack of *All About Eve*? No way. Professor Faraci had canceled out and she'd come over to the show by herself and just run into Brendan at the candy counter and asked if she could sit with him because his suit was so attractive? Not likely. And beyond these pitiful lies — which would never work in a million years — she couldn't think of any others. She was really in the soup.

"Hi, Dad. Hi, Martine," she said cheerily, hoping for a miracle. But none was coming her way.

"Young lady," her father started, and from there she knew this conversation was going to go downhill. Whenever parents began the sentence with "Young lady," nothing good *ever* followed.

At midnight, after her dad and Martine were asleep, Stacy sat in the dark in the den and punched out her own phone number. It was only ten in California and Alix would still be up.

"Hi," she whispered when her sister answered.

"Stacy!" Alix shouted excitedly.

"Shhh, don't let Mom know I'm calling."

"How's it going?"

"Oh, just great. I've only been here three days, and I've totally ruined your life."

Alix started laughing on the other end.

"This is no laughing matter," Stacy insisted. "You've got a boyfriend."

"I do? But that sounds like *good* news."

"Well, it basically is except that he thinks

you're a compulsive liar. Plus you're grounded for a week because you snuck out on a date with him."

"I snuck out on a date. But I don't even have dates! Wow, I sound kind of wild. I think I like this new me. You're probably going to hate the new you."

"Well, you've got to do better at geometry than I could."

"I haven't even started summer school yet. Right now I'm just making a total mess of your personal life. Your boyfriend is in a rage. He's probably just about to break up. And you had a terrible fight where you insulted your best friend."

"Rosalie?"

"You said you didn't like her all that much anyway," Alix teased.

"Al — "

"Okay, okay, I'll straighten everything out," she said, then added weakly, "somehow."

"Oh, I know you will. But now tell me how you got into all this trouble in the first place."

"Well, it all started earlier tonight in the Big Boy parking lot. . . ."

Chapter 11

This is how Alix managed to have a huge fight with Rosalie *and* get Sam mad at her — all in one night.

Sam had come by for her around seven-thirty. She thought they were actually going somewhere, like on a date. To the movies, to a party, maybe. But Sam just drove into town and pulled into the Big Boy parking lot. Some of the other kids from the pool party were there hanging out, sitting on the hoods of their cars, or with their legs dangling out the backs of their vans or Ranchers or Blazers. They were talking in small groups, eating burgers, sipping shakes.

It looked to Alix like a gathering of the wagons before the wagon train headed west. Only no one here in the Big Boy lot seemed to be going anywhere.

Alix felt like one of those anthropologists studying the customs of some strange jungle tribe. Back in Chicago, the kids at the conservatory who were more social than she was — that is to say the kids who were not terminally shy — went on dates. They *did* things together. Went to movies, plays, concerts. To the festivals held in the park. Or out to dinner at cheap ethnic restaurants.

Here in Joshua Tree, the main activity seemed to be hanging out, and the high school kids had perfected it to an art. Who you hung out with was very significant. Alix could see that Stacy ran with the coolest crowd — all the lettermen and class officers and cheerleaders. This crowd's hangout was the Big Boy. Part of hanging out here involved making fun of a less cool group — the "Donuts," who hung out at Dan's Donuts down the street. Even lower on the scale were the "Trippers." Alix figured out they were the kids who studied and got grades and went to the library and worse, signed up for the field trips offered at school — the kids she, Alix, would probably fit in with best.

"I mean, who wants to go all the way in to L.A. to go to some stupid art museum?" Rosalie was saying now, talking about the last field trip she'd skipped. She and Alix were sitting together on the hood of Sam's car. Rosalie was filing her nails. From what Alix could tell, Rosalie devoted the bulk of her free time to personal beauty rituals, even managing to work them into her social life. Like now, there was a bottle of nail polish stuck in the breast pocket of her bleached denim jacket, and so the filing was probably just a prelim to the main event of the night for her.

"I kind of like art museums," Alix said.

Rosalie crossed her eyes and said, "Ugh. We've got about all the art I can stand just around my house — what with all those shell mosaics my sister does. You know, like the monkey in the clown suit. And even that's better than the stuff they saw at that dumb museum. Remember the pictures in the school paper? Those sculptures that looked like car wrecks? That painting that was all one color? Like, give me a break."

"That's *modern* art," Alix said.

"Hunh?" Rosalie said. She always wore her Walkman, but kept the sound low enough so she could hear the conversation — except when a George Michael song came on. Then she'd roll the volume up to the limit. George Michael must be on now, Alix guessed, and so decided to drop her art lecture. It would be useless anyway. Rosalie was the kind of person who didn't want to know anything she didn't already know. Alix wondered how she could be Stacy's best friend.

Still, there *was* something she wanted to talk with Rosalie about. Kissing. Having gone with Mike for so long, Ro had probably done a lot of kissing and might be able to give Alix some tips on whipping Sam into shape. But before George Michael was gone from Rosalie's airwaves, Mike and Sam were coming out of the Big Boy, carrying white paper sacks toward the car.

"Fries, m'lady?" Mike said, bowing from the waist in front of Rosalie, offering her the open bag.

"I'll pass. Today is the first day of the rest of my diet," Rosalie said.

"I'll take a few," Sam said, and went to reach into the bag. But Mike was too fast. He pulled it away and took off, jumping over the hoods of a couple of cars. Sam ran after him.

"Guys," Rosalie said, rolling her eyes.

"So you're on a diet?" Alix said.

"I'm pretty much always on a diet. At least for *part* of the day."

"How much do you want to lose — fifty?" Alix was only making what she thought was an accurate guess, but Rosalie's eyes went stone cold.

"Thanks," she said, her voice dripping with sarcasm. "What're friends for, eh?"

"Oh Rosalie, I'm — " Alix started to say, but Rosalie stopped her with a raised hand. She started talking, not directly to Alix, but to some imaginary audience of sympathetic friends.

"I mean really. Five pounds? Ten maybe? Nooooo. Stacy doesn't think that's even close. No, I need to drop fifty. The implication? That I am a blimp, a pork chop."

Alix knew she'd really goofed. She'd been about as insulting as Martine. The major leagues. She tried desperately to think of something to say to smooth things over and wound up blurting out, "I only thought that, if you lost a whole bunch of weight, it would distract people from looking at your braces."

As soon as the words were out of her mouth, even before she saw Rosalie's eyes bug out with rage, Alix knew she'd really done it — entered the Martine Hall of Fame.

She didn't dare risk saying anything else. Who knows what might come out of her mouth? She was beginning to feel like the girl in *The Exorcist*. She stood in mortified silence as Rosalie jumped off the hood of the car and grabbed Mike by the elbow and practically dragged him over to his jeep. As she watched them drive off, she suddenly felt The Arm descend on her shoulder. Sam.

"What kind of fire did you light under her?"

"Oh. Don't ask. Sometimes I am the most tactless person on the planet."

"You? Stacy Wyatt? Miss Congeniality of Joshua Tree? You've got to be kidding. Ro was probably just in a foul mood. She probably saw Mike sharing his fries with Sonia Brown."

"Is Mike interested in . . . Sonia?"

"Well, you know Sonia."

Of course, Alix didn't know Sonia from a sack of fries. Stacy's briefings were beginning to show a lot of gaps.

"Just how do you mean?" Alix tried prompting Sam.

"Well, Sonia's such a goddess type — so ungettable. I suppose every guy in school — even us old 'married men' have to wonder what it would be like to be the one who finally catches Queen Sonia. I don't know if anything's going on between her and Mike, but I do know — and so does Rosalie — that if anyone else could get him, it would be Sonia. So it probably wasn't what you said to her — or *only* what you said — that got her so hopping mad. I think she wanted an excuse to get Mike out of here pronto! Which reminds me . . ."

Alix felt The Arm give her shoulders a meaningful squeeze and looked up to see Sam looking down at her affectionately. This was his best expression and made him look cuter. Still not "hunk," but less "hulk."

"So?" he said.

"Hunh?" she said, still not getting the message.

"Want to go for a little desert ride?"

Around Joshua Tree, "desert ride" was a kind of code for parking out on some deserted piece of scrubland. In this specific case, "desert ride" meant she'd have to kiss Sam again.

Argh, she thought, but smiled sweetly and got into his car beside him. It looked like she wasn't going to get any tips from Rosalie, at least not tonight. She was going to have to give Sam his first kissing lesson all on her own. She gulped and prepared herself.

She didn't have much time, though. Sam was not big on build-up. There were no violins on the soundtrack of his movie. What he did was stop the car, cut the engine, turn to Alix and say, "You really look great tonight." And then he pounced.

Alix pulled back.

"Uh, Sam."

"Yeah?"

"Did you ever think of doing this with a little less . . . well, pressure?"

"What pressure? I thought you said you wanted to come out here?"

"No, I meant kissing pressure. You mash my mouth."

"I *mash* your mouth?" He pulled back against his side of the door and looked a little shocked.

She nodded.

"That's just passionate."

"No," Alix said, then couldn't resist adding, "it's *mash*-ionate." She couldn't help giggling at her dumb joke, but soon noticed she was the only one laughing.

"Why didn't you ever tell me this before?" Sam said in a hurt voice.

"I was working up to it."

"Working up to it? *For a year?* For a year you've been hating my kissing and waiting to tell me? Probably telling all your stupid girl-friends, though. I can just hear you all in the girls' john. They probably call me Sam the Masher. I *thought* they were looking at me kind of funny at Bill's party."

"Come on," she tried to assure him. "I haven't told anyone."

"But you've been thinking it. Thinking I'm

some sort of make-out klutz. I'll have you know I kissed my share of girls around here before you, and I never had any complaints."

Alix sort of knew he wanted her to ask who all these girls were, but since she didn't care, she didn't bother.

"Uh," she said, trying to work this situation around to a more positive tack, "maybe I could show you what I mean?"

"Oh," he said in a stupid, fakey-sweet way that was pure sarcasm, "a little lesson. Thanks . . . but no thanks."

And with that, he turned the key in the ignition, turned the radio on to max volume, and headed out to the highway and back to town. The conversation was over.

When they got to her house, he just reached across and opened the passenger door, then sat like an exasperated school bus driver waiting for the slowpoke kid who'd lost a tennis shoe.

"Sam?" Alix tried to say, leaning back through the open window when she'd gotten out of the car.

"I'll call you," he said, put the car in reverse and backed out of the driveway and roared off down the street as a way of saying, "Who cares about you anyway?"

"Good work, Alix," she said aloud, standing in the middle of the driveway, miserable at the amount of damage she'd managed to do to Stacy's life in just one night. She shook her head at what a failure she was turning out to be at this. At this rate, she supposed she'd somehow manage to flunk geometry, too.

Chapter 12

They couldn't really ground Stacy entirely because, since her father and Martine thought she was Alix, she had to be allowed out for her violin lessons.

Boy, Stacy thought. If only they knew that Professor Faraci is thousands of miles away in sunny Italy, and Alix is thousands of miles away in sunny California, and that not even the violin is here in Chicago!

Luckily, violin lessons and getting all the way downtown and back to take them, took about three hours. After stashing the violin case and changing clothes, Stacy still had time for both a good run, and time left over to see Brendan. More and more, the "seeing Brendan" part was becoming the important part.

He wasn't like any guy she'd ever known. He was a total free spirit. He didn't follow any styles, didn't have any crowd. He didn't have any typical guy interests, like sports or cars. He read all the time — everything from novels to books on improving your memory to leaflets handed out by wild-eyed people on the streets. ("I like to keep up with the latest trends in craziness," he told her.)

This summer, he was teaching himself to type with a set of books and tapes. Plus he was building a radio from a kit. He wanted her to go see it that afternoon. She'd never been to his apartment, which was near Wrigley Field, the ballpark where the Chicago Cubs played. She was curious to see what his place would look like. He lived with his mother. She worked two jobs and was hardly ever home.

"I'm a 'latchkey child,' " he said as he let them in.

"You're too old to be a latchkey child," she told him. His parents had just gotten a divorce. From what Stacy could see as they walked in, it looked like his father must've gotten all the furniture.

In the living room, there were only some stereo components, a futon and a lawn chair. In the dining room, there was a card table and three mismatched chairs. Brendan's room, though, looked normal — well, normal for

Brendan. In addition to a dresser, pasted over with a million decals, and a set of bunk beds dripping with tangles of sheets and blankets (where Spot headed right away, settling into what was clearly his little place), there was a desk with a typewriter and tape recorder on it, and a work table in the center of the room. On it was "the radio."

"It doesn't really look like a radio," Stacy said. He was always completely honest with her, so she felt free to say what she really thought. "It looks like a miniature junk yard."

"I'm insulted. I'm following all the directions to a fault."

"Oh, yeah, sure. This here looks like a real standard part," she said, pointing to a purple Indian headdress feather soldered straight up out of one of the circuit boards.

"Oh. That's for good luck," he said. "I've got a feeling this is going to be a special radio, an exceptional radio. I think it's going to be able to pick up signals from other planets. Maybe other dimensions. Maybe other times — you know, past and future."

Stacy had to laugh.

"Nothing like aiming high," she said, and then, turning around, saw a huge wooden bookcase filled with hundreds of records — thick records not quite as big as albums, in paper sleeves rather than cardboard jackets. She pulled one out.

"Old 78s," Brendan explained. "Jazz and blues records from the thirties and forties. I pick them up in second-hand stores and old record shops."

"Wow. They're like non-compact discs. What do you play them on?"

He pointed to an ancient record player with three legs. The fourth corner was propped up on a rickety stack of books. He took the record out of her hand and put it on the turntable and switched the player on. The sound of scratches filled the room. Then, over them, came the most strange and wonderful voice. A woman singing out of some faraway past place.

"Wow," Stacy whispered.

"Yeah," Brendan said. "Billie Holiday."

"I never heard her before," Stacy admitted. "I guess I pretty much only listen to rock."

"I like rock, too," he said, flopping down next to Spot on the bottom bunk. "But there's other good stuff. You just have to look a little harder to find it."

One of the best parts about hanging out with Brendan was how he could show her a million new things without ever making her feel dumb for not knowing about them already. Now he leapt up, the dog following him out of the room. He said over his shoulder to Stacy, "Want a snack?"

"What've you got?"

He looked into the refrigerator. Spot stood behind him, tail wagging at the possibility of goodies.

"Let's see. Two onions, a jar of mint jelly, a head of lettuce from the Paleolithic Age and a magical mystery foil lump." He pulled this last item out and inspected it. Spot backed up. "Seems to be fur growing out of the side here. Think I should open it?"

"Not until the bomb de-detonators get here. And the toxic waste crew."

Brendan shut the refrigerator door dramatically, and leaned against it as if barricading the dangerous object inside. Then he said to Stacy in a weird accent, "Come with me, Igor. Out of my la-*bor*-a-tory. I will walk you through the forest to the castle."

And then he headed out of the apartment walking like a demented scientist with Spot behind him, looking a little like a demented dog. Stacy followed the two of them. Brendan kept up the mad scientist walk all the way down the stairs and out onto the street and down the blocks toward the park where she'd stashed the violin case. The longer he did it, the stupider the joke got, but for some reason, the funnier it struck Stacy. By the time they got into the park, she was laughing so hard her knees were weak. She leaned up against one of the big trees lining the running path. Brendan came over and leaned against another side of the tree and just stared toward the harbor.

At first Stacy thought he was just spacing, but then she began to feel a tenseness radiating out from him. As though he was wanting to say something, but couldn't find the words. Maybe it was something about his life. Maybe it had to do with his pitiful refrigerator. Maybe he and his mother were really poor. Maybe they'd been living on mint jelly for the past week.

"Alix?" he finally said. Stacy whirled around, looking for her sister. She still did this sometimes when her reflexes kicked in before she could remember *she* was supposed to be Alix.

"Hey," Brendan said, taking her hand, "What are you looking for? I'm trying to ask you an important question."

"Okay," she said. "Shoot."

"Do you like me?"

She burst out laughing with surprise. She couldn't help it. It was the last thing in the world she had expected him to say.

"Oh, no," he moaned. "It's not *that* hilarious, is it?"

"No, no, it's just that . . . well, of course I like you."

"But do you *really* like me?"

"Yes, I *really* like you."

"No, what I mean is, do you like me like a friend, or like a boyfriend?"

Stacy pretended to think about this for a moment, just to tease him, then said, "Definitely like a boyfriend."

"You do? Oh, that's great!" he shouted and started jumping up and down. Which started Spot jumping up and down, creating a small commotion that attracted the attention of everyone around them in the park.

And then he suddenly stopped jumping and was kissing her. It was very different from kissing Sam — different and better. Just thinking about Sam in comparison with Brendan only reminded her how little she'd thought of him since she'd come to Chicago, how little she missed him, how much the focus of her thoughts had shifted to Brendan.

The only bad thing about this terrific kiss was that they were interrupted in the middle of it.

"Alix Wyatt!"

She broke away from Brendan as though he were electrified and turned to see — of all people — Martine! She was on her racing bike.

Apparently she'd been cruising through the park on her afternoon ride and spotted Stacy and Brendan. Argh.

"I think you'd better come with me," Martine said to her in a strict voice.

Stacy nodded and squeezed Brendan's hand in a silent, dejected good-bye. She picked up the case and followed Martine glumly. Now she was probably never going to get to see him. Martine and her dad were probably going to keep her grounded for the rest of the summer, instead of letting her out on Saturday as they'd promised.

They walked in silence as they made their way south along the harbor. When Martine finally spoke, Stacy couldn't have been more surprised at what she said.

"I won't tell your dad."

"What?" said Stacy, incredulous. "I mean, thanks a lot, but why not?"

"Well," Martine said with a slight smile coming across her face. "One good thing about having a young stepmother is that I'm not all that far from fifteen myself. I remember what it was like to be grounded. It drove me crazy. I always felt like I had to break out — and usually did. And . . . well, I can also remember kissing my first curly-haired boy. I don't want to be the wicked stepmother who spoils that moment for you."

"Martine."

"Hmm?"

Stacy wanted to give her a hug, but couldn't quite get there. Instead, she just said, "Thanks. A lot."

"No problem. Say, want to stop at that little gazebo place for an ice cream? I've been having the most incredible cravings for ice cream lately." She smiled and patted her little stomach, indicating that the cravings were due to her being pregnant.

Maybe Martine wasn't such a bad egg after all. Maybe there was hope for her and Alix getting along. Maybe she was making some progress toward solving Alix's problems. Martine. Brendan. The problem with Brendan, though, was that Stacy was having a harder and harder time remembering that he was supposed to be *Alix's* new boyfriend, not her own.

Chapter 13

Alix was almost out the door of remedial geometry when Mr. Henley called and asked her to please stay behind for a minute.

"Stacy. I'm amazed at this first quiz of yours. A perfect score. The highest grade in the class. What's *happened* to you since spring?"

"Well, Mr. Henley, the break gave me some time to do a little serious thinking. To ask myself some hard questions. Stacy, I said to myself, what are the important things in life? Parties? Boys? Hanging out at the Big Boy? Or is the important thing in life of the mind? Sitting in the quiet of the library. Reading. Doing geometry. Anyway, it became clear to me that I had to knuckle down and apply myself to the things that mattered. And as you can see. . . ." She held up the quiz he'd just handed back in class.

"Stacy. I'm very impressed with this new attitude of yours."

"Thank you, Mr. Henley. Actually, it was mostly due to you that I got myself on the right track."

"Me?"

"Yes, you and your love of geometry. It made me see that there was a fascinating new world out there in numbers." While Alix could barely make conversation with anyone her own age, years of being an A-student had made her an ace at soft-soaping teachers and had led her to a crucial discovery: No matter how cool a teacher might be in the rest of his life, when it came to *his* subject, he always felt it was just about the most fascinating and under-appreciated subject on earth. There was nothing you could say in praise of it that would sound ridiculous or overboard to him. Mr. Henley only proved this point. He was sort of glowing by the time Alix walked out of his classroom.

Of course, this is probably the *only* good thing I'm doing here for Stacy, she thought on the way to her locker. She undid the lock and pulled out a big hiking backpack, the only thing she'd been able to find in Stacy's closet big enough to hold her violin.

She'd found a place to practice undiscovered,

undisturbed. In the desert just outside town there was a small grove of Joshua trees — maybe the grove that gave the town its name for all she knew. In the center there was a clearing with a rock-lined pit. For campfires and cookouts, she guessed. But all the times she'd come here during the day, it had been deserted.

And so she took her bike (Stacy's bike, really, although she was beginning to think of a lot of Stacy's stuff as hers) and headed through town. Just as she got to where the stores ended and the desert began, she saw Mike Beal's jeep heading into town, toward her. Rosalie was sitting in the passenger seat and Alix waved, but Rosalie stared ahead stonily, as though she hadn't seen her. The big frosty.

Rosalie hadn't spoken to her since that night at the Big Boy. Sam had called once, but just to stay good-bye before he left on the wilderness trek. He'd been cool and formal. Alix could tell it was a duty call. He said he'd call when he got back, that he had some "heavy thinking" to do out in the woods. He made this sound as ominous as possible, so she knew he was thinking about breaking up. He was supposed to have gotten back to town yesterday, but so far the phone hadn't rung.

Alix had two sets of emotions about this. One side of her heart felt terrible that she might have ruined this romance for Stacy. The other side, though, said her sister could do better than this lunk with the dead-weight arm and possessive nature. Stacy herself had complained about Sam's limitations. Maybe Alix was doing her a favor by getting rid of him for Stacy. Then when she came back here, she'd be free to find some guy who was less of a Neanderthal.

She got to the grove and swung herself off the bike, then leaned it up against the trunk of one of the trees. She was beginning to find some things about living in California that she liked a lot more than living in the city. This little private place was one of those things. She'd almost never played her violin outside a practice room or concert hall before. Playing outdoors was a weird and kind of wonderful experience. The music felt like it was lifting off the strings and sailing up toward the clouds.

She tuned the violin now, put rosin on her bow, then began to play the Paganini Violin Concerto No. 1. She just called this Number One, because it was her personal favorite among all the pieces for violin. She stood in the center of the clearing, sunlight coming down on her in broad shafts. The few birds in the branches stopped singing and just stood still, listening.

As Alix played, she went into something close to a trance. She wasn't in the desert, or in the Joshua tree grove, she was inside the music.

And so she didn't hear anyone come up through the trees, didn't see anyone standing in the shadows listening along with the birds. Finally, when she played the last, climactic notes, and brought her violin out from between her chin and shoulder, she stood still for a moment in the aftermath of the music. It was then that she heard the twig crunching under a footstep.

She turned sharply, frightened. And then exhaled with relief when she saw who it was.

"Sam. You scared me. B-b-but how . . . ?"

"I was looking for you. Your mom said you were at school, but by the time I got there, class had let out. Then I ran into Mike and Ro, and they said they'd seen you heading this way. Once I got into the desert, I started to hear the music and followed it. Gee, Stacy, I didn't even know you were musical. I thought your sister was the one who played the violin."

"Uh," Alix said, hunting for a response, "yeah, well, she taught me while we were together down at my Gram's."

"You learned to play like that in two weeks?"

"Well," Alix said, telling what was probably the single biggest lie of her life, "it's really pretty easy to play the violin. Especially if you use these little color-coded tabs under the strings. You start with easy stuff like 'I'm a Little Bunny' and pretty soon, you're up to Paganini."

"Boy," he said, shaking his head, taking the violin from her and plucking at the strings. "Maybe you could teach me. I'm actually pretty musical. I used to play the triangle in my grade school band."

The triangle! Alix thought. Now there's a toughy. She couldn't keep from laughing, at the image of Sam with his triangle, and even funnier at the image of him playing a delicate violin.

"What's so funny?" Sam asked.

"Nothing," she said and covered her mouth in spite of knowing it was stupid, that someone could always see you laughing behind your hand.

"You know," Sam said, "I'm tired of everyone thinking that just because I'm big, I can't be sensitive or artistic or gentle. Big guys get a bum rap. Arnold Schwarzenegger — I'll bet he's an incredibly sensitive guy. Probably does all the housework for his wife. Big guys don't have to prove to anyone that they're not wimps. They can just relax and be sensitive. Or at least they could if everyone wasn't always assuming they're just insensitive jerks."

For a second, Alix didn't know what to say. She was really surprised to hear that Sam had thoughts like these.

"But," she said when she'd thought about this for a minute, "how can you be sensitive — or even *think* you're sensitive — when so much of the time you *do* act like an insensitive . . . well, an insensitive jerk?"

"What?" he sputtered, his face flushing red up to the roots of his thick, straw-colored hair.

"Well, you do have sort of a caveman approach to girls, to me. I mean, you never ask where I want to go or what I want to do. You just drag me along like a cave wife. And then when we get there, you act like I'm your possession — like a set of golf clubs you've brought and have to keep an eye on." She decided to skip the part about The Arm. She could see from his expression that he was already bristling at all this criticism.

"Not to mention my face-mashing kissing," he said sarcastically.

This wasn't working. He was just getting madder. She should probably just back down, tell him he was a great guy and leave him for

Stacy to deal with when she got back. What did she care if he went rolling over life like a tank? He wasn't *her* boyfriend.

And so she tried to come up with something calming, something to fluff up his injured feelings. But she couldn't. Couldn't think of anything to say, and couldn't bring herself to lie. And so for a long moment, the two of them just stood facing each other in silence against the sounds of the desert. Alix expected him to either turn and storm off, or else say something cutting. And so she was totally surprised when he broke the silence by saying, "I can kiss better. I've been thinking about it. And practicing."

"Practicing how?"

"Kissing the back of my hand."

"Your hand?" Alix said and nearly laughed again trying to picture this.

"Well, first I tried kissing a peach, but that way only the peach knew how I was doing." By then he was laughing, too. And then all of a sudden neither of them was laughing and Alix was feeling distinctly nervous, but didn't know why.

"So? Want to give me a try?" he asked. "You can rate me — one to ten. So I know how I'm doing."

"Okay," Alix said and closed her eyes and

kissed the new Sam. In a word, it was fabulous — everything she'd always imagined kissing would be. But wait, she told herself. This guy is Stacy's boyfriend, not yours. She thought about this for a few seconds, then pushed the thought gently out of her head. Then she opened her eyes, and saw Sam looking at her intently.

"Well?"

Alix the Kissing Judge deliberated for an instant, then said, "Nine and a half."

"Only nine and a half?"

"Well, I want to leave room for more improvement . . . and more practicing," she said and closed her eyes again.

Chapter 14

Some days the "switch" was a breeze for Stacy. She'd gotten to know where everything was around the apartment. The first week she figured she must have looked dyslexic, reaching for a plate to put her sandwich on and opening the glass cabinet by mistake. Taking the glass over to where she thought the soda was kept and pulling out a giant bottle of Clorox.

By now, though, she had the basics down pat, which made most of being Alix easy. Most, but not quite all. The hardest part was pretending to have all of Alix's interests. Unfortunately, she had what seemed like a million of them — all deep and intellectual. She was always reading. And not just *People* or *Seventeen*. Books. And not just romances, but heavy-duty *literature*. Classics. Which Stacy now had to sit around reading. Actually, some of them weren't as bad as she'd expected.

The worst thing was having to pretend to be crazy about classical music, which actually *drove* her crazy. It made her brain circuits feel like they were shorting out. So she developed this little system: She put on Vivaldi or Mozart nice and quiet on the stereo in her room. Then put her Walkman headphones on and turned the volume so it was just enough to drown out the classical under a wave of rock.

The toughest situation — and the one she still hadn't found a way out of yet — was talking with her dad and Martine, who liked to quiz Alix on all her intellectual pursuits. While this was probably great for Alix, it made Stacy feel like she was in the interrogation room in the police station, being grilled.

Like tonight. The three of them were having dinner at the deli near their apartment. It was Saturday and they were eager to hear about her Impressionists lecture at the Art Institute that afternoon. Actually, Stacy had gone to a Cubs game with Brendan. Neither of them knew the first thing about the game, but he'd brought along a book on baseball from the library and they'd had fun figuring it out in a backward kind of way. This afternoon of fooling around though, while it had been great fun, had left her extremely low on facts about the art lecture.

"Which painters did the professor talk about this time?" her father asked as he spread applesauce over his potato pancakes.

"Oh," Stacy said, picking at the little cup of cole slaw next to her pastrami sandwich. "All of them."

"Manet?"

"Oh, yeah. Well, of course. What would the Impressionists be without Manet, right?"

"What about Monet?" Who? Sounded an awful lot like Manet. She hoped like crazy she wasn't going to have to tell them apart.

"Well, sure," she said. "Monet and Manet and . . ."

"Degas."

"Right."

"How do you like the paintings?" Martine asked.

"Oh, I do. Sure. They're so . . ." she desperately tried to think of something that would be sure to be right. ". . . so colorful." All paintings had color, she figured and was pretty pleased with herself.

"What about their use of light?" her dad asked.

"Oh, I think they pretty much had to sit by

the window when they painted. They didn't have much electricity back then." As soon as she'd said this, the "wrong" buzzer went off inside her head, like on a TV game show.

"I was referring to the innovative ways the Impressionists painted light — coming through trees, reflecting off the water," her dad said. "Surely he must have brought this up in his lectures." The way he said it, though, Stacy could tell what he really meant was that he knew she wasn't going to the lectures. How much else did he know? How long would it take for him to put the pieces together and figure out what she and Alix were doing? And how mad would he be?

She was very relieved when Martine changed the subject to the baby's room. They were going to convert the den into a nursery, and were trying to come up with the right color.

"Not pink or blue," Stacy's dad said. "Everybody does that."

"And not yellow, just because I hate yellow," Martine said.

"What about peach?" Stacy suggested. "It's pretty, non-sexist, and it's restful."

"Peach?" her father said. "I think she's got it."

Stacy was flattered that they were consulting her on stuff like this. It clearly meant they intended to include Alix in their new family. She had to remember to tell Alix she wouldn't be living in the elevator.

About a week later, Martine surprised Stacy by asking her if she wanted to go shopping.

"This kid is getting so big, I'm popping out of even my baggiest outfits. I guess I'm going to have to break down and actually buy some maternity clothes." Martine was a penny pincher, and it was bugging her that she was going to have to spend money on clothes she'd only be wearing for a few months. But now she'd heard about a second-hand maternity shop, and this is where she and Stacy headed.

"The Thrifty Stork," Stacy read the sign in the window. She and Martine went in and began going through the racks of clothes.

"Not too much here that's what you'd call hip," Stacy observed. "Basically polka dots and gingham checks."

"I guess this is the only kind of stuff they make for pregnant women," Martine said. "It's funny. I always saw expectant mothers wearing these clothes and I thought it must be that when you get pregnant, something happens to your hormones and it affects your sense of style. Suddeny you want to go around in pastels, looking like one of those ceramic Hummel figures."

Stacy burst out laughing. When she relaxed a little, Martine was actually pretty witty.

"*Voilà!*" Stacy said, holding up a plain navy cotton dress with a large center pleat in front.

"Oh, nice," Martine said, feeling the fabric. They poked around some more and found two tops and a pair of maternity jeans with an elastic panel in front. In the fitting room, Stacy noticed Martine's rounded stomach.

"Yup," Martine said, patting it. "Little Horace or Edwina." Although Stacy still had trouble believing it, these were the names Martine had picked out. They were old names from her family or something, but still . . . the poor kid. And it was then that, for the first time, the fact of this baby really sunk in. This baby was related to her, part of the same family as her and Alix. Their little half sister or brother.

"It's kind of exciting, isn't it?" she said to Martine, then realized this sounded dopey. "I guess that's the understatement of the year."

"No, I know what you mean. I hadn't really thought much about being a mother, but when Steve and I got married, we both knew almost right away that we wanted to have a baby together. It's like you fall in love with someone and there's so much love between the two of you that it sort of spills over and you want to create someone out of all that extra love."

"You two are really happy together, aren't you?" Stacy asked, handing Martine one of the sleeveless tops.

"Oh, yeah."

"Martine?" Stacy said, then waited until Martine's head popped out of the neck hole of the top.

"Yes?"

"Do you know why it didn't work out for my mom and dad?"

Martine pulled her hair back off her face with both hands and stood for a moment looking like she was trying to put a complicated thought into words.

"I know they were real young when they met. In high school. They went through college together and got married right after that. People change, though. Over the years, I think they just gradually stopped loving each other. Sometimes the person who's absolutely perfect for you at fifteen is the absolutely wrong person for you at forty. Do you know what I mean?"

Do I ever! Stacy thought, flashes of Sam, then Brendan rushing through her mind. Sometimes the absolutely right person for you at fourteen is the wrong one at *fifteen*!

Chapter 15

Alix was filling the dishwasher after Sunday dinner. Out the window over the sink, she could see her mother and Alan Sakamoto working on phase one of the Japanese fern garden they were putting in the backyard. When it was done, it was even going to have a little goldfish pond. Alan was becoming a part of their lives.

At first, Alix had felt some of the same sort of resentment toward him that she had toward Martine. But he'd worn down her resistance. Mostly with his mega-weird sense of humor. There were his terrible puns. And then there were his practical jokes. He bought a gizmo — a little microphone — that hooked up to the TV set, and once when Alix was watching, during a pause between a program and a commercial, this serious voice came out of the TV saying, "Stacy Wyatt — why are you watching me instead of doing your geometry homework?" She just about fell off the couch. *The Voice of Doom!* But then she spotted Alan around the corner leading into the hallway, doubling over, cracking up. She ran out and jumped on his back and began pummeling him.

"Help!" he screamed for Alix's mother. "Teen-Age Girl Attack!"

Worse (better?) yet, was the day the doorbell rang and Alix answered and there was Alan, dressed in a Santa suit. She burst out laughing and let him in. He flopped onto the sofa in mock depression.

"Oh, yeah. Everybody loves Santa when it's Christmas. But when he doesn't have any presents and it's the middle of July and he stops by for a glass of iced tea and a little conversation, then they just laugh in his face. Well, just remember young lady — even in the summer, he's still making his list and checking it twice. He's still going to find out who's naughty and nice."

"You going to marry Alan?" she asked her mother later that night as Alix went into her room where her mother was in bed reading.

Karen Wyatt just looked up and said mysteriously, "That's for me to know and you to find out." Then she burst out in giggles. Alix had no choice but to jump in bed and begin tickling her. Her mother was helpless at the mercy of a tickler.

"Boy," Alix said as they both gasped with laughter, "I can't wait to grow up and become an adult so I can say really mature things like, 'That's for me to know and you to find out.'"

"Do you like him?" her mother asked.

"Yeah," Alix had to admit. "His puns are pretty terrible, though. And he's not as cute as Dad."

She was torn in her thinking about Alan and her mother. On the one hand, she had to admit that her mother seemed happier with him than she'd been in a long time. On the other hand, if they got married, that put yet another obstacle in the path of Alix's master plan (a plan she hadn't given up on in spite of what Stacy and Gram said) — getting her mother and father and her and Stacy back together again. One big, happy family.

Well, one medium-sized, kind of happy family anyway. She could still remember the way her mother was always disappointed in her dad for being away so much. And the way he was silent so much of the time when he was around the house. Still, she figured they could work out their problems if they could just get back together again. She knew this dream was pretty far-fetched, but that didn't stop her from having it.

The next afternoon, she was thinking about her dream again when she was interrupted by the ringing of the yellow wall phone by the refrigerator.

"Alix?"

"Stacy! How's it going?"

"Just what I was calling to ask you. How's geometry?"

"Well," Alix said. "All I need to know is if you want an A or a B."

"What? I have a choice?"

"Sure. I can get you an A, but that might look suspicious. Maybe you want me to get a nice, safe B."

"No way," Stacy said, laughing. "After all the agony I went through for geometry, I deserve at least an A."

"It's as good as done. How's Martine? Have you tamed the Wicked Witch of the Midwest for me?"

"Oh, she's not so bad," Stacy said.

"Come on," Alix said. "Get real."

"No, really. She told me the other day that she's been scared of me — that is, of *you*."

"Me? But why?"

"Well, I think she thinks you don't like her.

She's the outsider in the situation. And you can keep her shut out. I think she picked up right away on your opinion of her and got defensive."

"But *she's* the one who insults me!"

"Alix. The woman is a social dolt. Martine could insult a lamp post if she stood next to it for fifteen minutes. But look, in the clutch she's great. Right now she's helping me — you — in the cause of true love." She told Alix about the time Martine caught her and Brendan in the park.

"Tell me more about Brendan. I still have trouble imagining him."

"*I* have trouble imagining him, and I see him practically every day. He's like a package of a million surprises." She found herself smiling as she said this, then suddenly not wanting to say anymore about him. More and more, she found herself thinking of Brendan and her, Stacy. Not Brendan and Alix. Supposedly she'd picked Brendan specifically for Alix. But now she didn't want to let him go. And she couldn't think of a way to talk to Alix about this. She didn't want to disappoint her after building her hopes up. She would — like it or not — simply have to stick to her bargain and turn Brendan over when the time came. But right now, she just didn't want to have to think about it. So she changed the subject. "Speaking of true love, is Sam still mad at you — at me?"

"Oh, no," Alix admitted. "He's come around." She started to tell Stacy about the kissing lessons and their afternoons out at the Joshua tree grove, but then she didn't. She wasn't sure why.

"So you've shaped him up," Stacy said. "And Mr. Henley. Next thing you tell me is you've got Rosalie signed up for Weight Watchers and she's grateful for your guidance."

"Not quite. She's still not speaking to me. I'll see her tonight, though. At the Mesa Fire."

"Oh," Stacy sighed. "There's going to be a Mesa Fire tonight? You're making me homesick. I'm just going to some stupid French restaurant with Dad and Martine."

"Mmmm. French food. I could kill for some paté. I've noticed that out here 'gourmet dining' means a restaurant with a salad bar."

"Joshua Tree has other charms."

"I know. More and more I'm seeing that. But I guess I'm still a city girl at heart."

"Not me. I love the action level, but I hate all the car fumes and the traffic and the noise."

"Well," Alix said. "I guess we'll both be glad to get back to our real lives in a couple of weeks then." She could hear the emptiness in her voice. And in Stacy's too when she said, "Yeah, it'll be great to go home. I can't wait."

Each of them *did* want to get back to her own life, but each also had a reason for wanting to stay where she was. Stacy's reason was Brendan. Alix's was — and no one could have been more surprised at this than her — Sam! The twins had started the summer with a big secret from everyone else. Now they each had a secret from the other.

Chapter 16

Stacy was on her way out of the apartment when she passed the living room and her father called out, "Alix, can I see you for a minute?"

She went in and flopped down onto the sofa across from where he was reading.

"You rang?" she said, impersonating the butler in this old movie she and Brendan had seen the other night at the Music Box.

"I was just wondering how your violin lessons were coming along this summer. You haven't said much about them lately."

"Oh, well, they're going fine. You know how it is with violin lessons. You rub the bow back and forth. Music comes out. There's really not much to say about it. Professor Faraci's still a great teacher — "

"He must be, considering. . . ."

"Uh, considering what?"

"Considering he's on another continent. This came for you today." He flipped a color postcard picturing the LaScala Opera House in Milan onto the coffee table between them.

"Ooops," Stacy said, twisting her mouth around in embarrassment at getting caught. Clearly her dad had figured out what she and Alix had done. Their cover was blown. The switch was over. She was just about to rush into an explanation of why they'd done it when he put up his hand to stop her.

"Please. Don't say anything. I already feel sorry enough."

"You do? But — "

"No. Don't try to make me feel better. I am completely in the wrong and that's that. I've simply put you under too much pressure. You're not a violin-playing machine or a junior adult. And so you had to go and duck out of your lessons and art lectures. Plainly this shows that what you really need is to be a regular teen-age girl. You need to not be so completely goal-oriented. You need to be aimless and worthless. You need to read trashy magazines about the personal lives of soap opera stars. You need to wear dimestore makeup. You need a goofy boyfriend with ears that stick out."

"They don't stick out *that* much," she said in

defense of Brendan. But her dad wasn't really listening. He was on a roll, leaning back in his reading chair, waving his hand in the air.

"Go out and have your fun. Take the rest of the summer off from that fiddle — and those lectures. You don't have to lie about anything to me anymore. Now I know your secret, and I understand." He leaned forward to look at her earnestly.

Not quite, you don't, Stacy thought while she was trying to look back at him with just as much earnestness.

"Thanks, Dad," she said in her most sincere voice, all the while feeling like a giant crumb. But then along with feeling like a crumb, she also felt relieved that she wouldn't have to lug Alix's stupid violin case around with her anymore. And on top of everything else, she felt exhilarated that they hadn't been caught, that the switch was still on. There was something incredibly, indescribably fun about fooling everyone.

"Well," she said, getting up and stretching and yawning and trying to look like she was just leaving casually. "I guess I'd better go find something worthless and adolescent to do."

"That's the idea," her father said. He was always fast to get into jokes and teasing. "Stay shy of armed robbery if you can. Maybe you could just bleach your hair some hideous color."

Stacy snapped her fingers.

"*Good* idea."

Stacy walked out of the apartment and onto the street, stopping to speak to Edward.

"Hey, Edward!" she said and gave him a high five.

"Alix," he said in his laid-back hippie voice, "You know, you are definitely changing in some inscrutable way. I can't put my finger on what it *is* that's different about you. . . ."

"My karma," she said. She walked on, leaving him to think about it.

As she walked she reached into the breast pocket of her short-sleeved sweatshirt and pulled out a small wad of cash. Alix's savings. She'd said for Stacy not to use it except in an emergency. But now there was one. Brendan's mother had lost her main job. Now all she had left was some part-time word processing, and that wasn't going to be enough to support the two of them. Her husband had flown the coop, so there wasn't going to be any help from him.

Brendan had been trying to contribute some of his own earnings. He was still too young to get a real job, but he'd put up signs on the bulletin boards in the local supermarkets.

HANDY BOY

Mows lawns.
Paints walls.
Walks dogs.
Sits babies.

He'd gotten a few jobs this way, but still, it wasn't enough to make a dent in their growing stack of bills. The last time Stacy stopped by, both Brendan and his mother were eating Twinkies and listening to old blues records. Sure signs of depression.

She tried to think of a way to cheer them up and finally came up with the brilliant idea of fixing them a "millionaire's dinner." It would take nearly every penny of Alix's savings and all of Stacy's kitchen creativity, but she was pretty sure she could pull it off. She was itching to do some cooking anyway. Alix didn't like to cook, so Stacy had to bury her talents all summer and eat either the carryout her Dad and Martine ordered, or the health food Martine kept the kitchen stocked with, which was a little too much like a horse putting on a feed bag to suit her.

Tonight was her night to shine, and to help two sad friends lighten up a little.

Her first stop was Treasure Island, the gourmet grocery store. She went through, carefully checking off each item on her list. Three little rainbow trout for her "trout almondine." Asparagus, butter, lemons, and eggs for her "asparagus hollandaise." A jar of el-cheapo caviar and sour cream and cute little white crackers for an appetizer. She even found sparkling apple juice in a wine bottle with a plastic cork that would pop like champagne.

When she got to the checkout and found she still had ten dollars to spare, she ran back and grabbed a small bouquet of flowers (the festive touch!) and walked out of the store smiling with anticipation.

There was one sad thing about this dinner, although only she knew it. In a way, it was a farewell celebration. Alix was coming home in a week and Stacy was determined — in spite of her own feelings — to turn Brendan over to her. And so this — although he wouldn't know it — was one of the last times they'd see each other.

She felt the beginnings of tears behind her eyes as she walked along carrying the sack of groceries.

I've got to toughen myself up, she thought. Stop being a wimp about this. She tried to think of all Brendan's bad points — all the things about him that she *wouldn't* miss. How his curly hair stuck out every which way. How he had no follow-through, starting a million projects and finishing none. How he was totally unathletic. She remembered the time she tried to take him running with her. To get to the running track, they had to go under a viaduct and by the time they got to the top of the steps on the way out, he was already panting and through for the day.

"But we're not even to the track yet," she'd protested.

"Sorry. I'll have to work up to it gradually, I guess. I don't think this is too bad for the first day, do you?"

She'd cracked up then and had to smile again even now just thinking of it. He was so cute and funny. She stopped herself in mid-thought. Clearly this — thinking of his bad points — wasn't going to work. Even his bad points were adorable.

She got to his apartment and rang the bell. Brendan answered the door and she pushed past him.

"Alix?" Brendan's mother, Barbara, said with surprise as she looked up from a travel brochure on Tahiti she was reading.

"Gourmet delivery service," Stacy said as

she bustled into the kitchen. All she had told them was to stay in tonight and not to fix dinner.

When Stacy had begun to set her ingredients out on the counter, Brendan pushed open the swinging door to the kitchen, trying to spy on what she was up to. But Stacy put a firm hand on his chest and shoved him right back out again.

"No one allowed in here except authorized personnel," she said.

"Just give me a rough idea of what's going on, and I promise I'll leave you alone."

"Well, let's just say that you really should be royalty because this is a dinner that's going to be fit for a king."

"Royalty, eh?" he said, as he backed out, thinking this over.

Stacy forgot all about him for the next hour. She was completely absorbed in preparing her feast, which turned out to be even more of a challenge than she expected. Brendan and his mother were of the "eggs and toast and canned soup" school of cooking. It was clear from the one saucepan and single cutting knife and the warped plastic spatula that Julia Child had never worked in their kitchen.

But, by rigging up one thing and another, being creative, and washing out the saucepan between each item she cooked in it, she managed to get the whole meal done. Then she set the old, formica-topped kitchen table with jelly jar glasses and dishtowels folded to look like napkins, and stuck the flowers into an old pitcher she found on a top shelf. She put out the bottle of sparkling juice and three wine glasses and then stood back and looked at her creation.

"Not bad," she said out loud to herself. She wiped her hands on a towel, smoothed back her hair and opened the door to call out, "Ladies and gentlemen, dinner is served."

She expected to surprise Brendan and his mother, but she didn't expect *them* to surprise *her*. They really did, though.

They came into the kitchen together.

"We thought as long as we were going to dine like royalty . . ." Brendan said.

". . . we'd better dress like them," his mom finished the sentence.

They stood side by side, dressed to the hilt — but what a hilt! Brendan had on a white tuxedo jacket so old it was yellow. Flowing out of the breast pocket was a ruby red silk handkerchief. Under the jacket, he was wearing a T-shirt with a bow tie printed on it. To complete the splendor of this outfit, he was wearing parachute pants.

His mother looked like a loony queen next to his mad prince.

"From my cameo performance as a bridesmaid," she said, gesturing at her floor-length pink satin gown. Her shoes, however, must have been from another celebration of the past. They were chartreuse.

"And, as queen," she added, "my crowning glory is . . . my crown." She tapped a fingernail against the tarnished tiara of rhinestones sitting at a jaunty angle on her head.

"You two!" Stacy exclaimed and doubled over laughing.

"We may ask you to sit in the scullery," Brendan said as he pulled out a chair for his mom.

"No, no, dear. We are easygoing royalty. We often permit the servants to dine with us. Especially when they've prepared a meal that looks like this. I mean, as you would say, Alix — wow!"

"How did you ever do this . . . in here?" Brendan said, truly amazed.

"Of course you know it's just the sort of thing I prepare for Brendan every night," his mother said.

"Yes," Brendan said. "We are very gourmet around here. I presume this will meet our usual standards."

The whole dinner was this silly — like the

Mad Hatter's tea party. Stacy couldn't remember a time when she'd had more fun. Brendan's mother, like Brendan, had a million different things she was interested in. One of her big things was being an "armchair traveler," which meant that although she never had the money to go anywhere, she still read tons of brochures and books about faraway places. She was so good at talking about these places, you almost forgot she hadn't been to any of them. She had that same easy, open way of talking about things that Brendan had. And also, like him, she just assumed that Stacy too had a million interesting things to talk about and fascinating opinions on every subject.

In her own family, Stacy had always been the outgoing, popular, athletic twin. Alix was the brainy, shy, cultured one. No one expected Stacy to have great thoughts on things. And so she mostly didn't. But with Brendan and his mother — because they assumed she had interesting things to say — she did. She found herself thinking of stuff ahead of time — subjects that interested her, curious stories out of the paper — to talk about with them. It was like, they just expected her to be this witty, fascinating person, and so she was.

She wondered how this witty, fascinating new Stacy would go over back in Joshua Tree.

Probably like a lead balloon. At least with Sam and Rosalie and most of the kids she hung out with. There were a few kids who might be fun. In her crowd, there was Mike Beals, Ro's boyfriend. He was on the debating team and into glider piloting. There were Jake Frey and Marilyn DeSanti. She'd done a science project with them last year. Their experiment had bombed, but the three of them still had a lot of fun. But then afterward, they'd all fallen back into their separate cliques. Jake and Marilyn were pretty much Trippers. They went for all the educational stuff her crowd made fun of. She'd have to take a lot of flak if she started hanging out with them. Still, it was probably better than spending the next two years watching Ro file her nails in the Big Boy parking lot.

It was funny. When Stacy had planned the switch with Alix, she'd only thought about the changes they'd be making in each other's lives. She hadn't thought of the possibility that the switch would change *her*.

Chapter 17

Stacy wasn't the only twin who was noticing changes in herself. The same night that she was fixing her royal supper for Brendan and his mother, Alix was going to the Mesa Fire with Sam.

She was getting ready in her room. (Well, it was really Stacy's room, but since she'd straightened it up a bit — organizing all the records alphabetically, sorting out the clothes in the closet by color, etc. — she felt more like it was her room. Her mother couldn't help noticing the rather dramatic change from the days when Stacy kept it just short of a Board of Health citation. When she asked, "What's come over you, Stacy?" Alix just replied, "Hormones."

Now she was standing in front of the mirror, trying on one of Stacy's better outfits — black stretch pants and a loose powder blue cotton sweater. She looked at her reflection in the mirror. She didn't look like the same person she was a few weeks ago. And it wasn't just that she was wearing Stacy's clothes. It was also that she was living Stacy's life.

Every morning, since she had to at least pretend to go out for a run, she had started actually doing some running. The first morning she'd only gone a couple of blocks before her lungs and legs began searing with pain. But she'd kept at it, going out each morning while the air off the desert was still cool. And by now she could run around the entire subdivision. She guessed this must be between a mile and a half and two miles.

She kept putting Sam off, though, for their Saturday morning runs. She could never make it four miles, and for sure not fast enough to look like Stacy. And so she just kept making up various pulled muscles and headaches and sudden errands for her mother. Sam said he didn't really care, that he was tired of getting beaten every time anyway.

He was turning out to be quite different from the person Alix had thought he was in the beginning, especially when he got away from his friends, when he didn't feel he had to be exactly like everybody else. It was when they were alone that he turned from strong silent type into practically a chatterbox. Now when they parked in the desert in his VW, they mostly talked. About everything and nothing — including a lot of things he'd never told Stacy.

He told her about his family, which had a lot of troubles. His older brother was in Juvenile Hall for stealing a car, and this was making his parents extra strict with Sam. He thought he wanted to become a doctor, but his dad wanted him to follow in his footsteps and be a carpenter. They didn't have much money, and so how was he going to ask them to put him through college and then medical school? He felt defeated before he even started.

Another surprise about him was how much he loved Alix's music. He often came out to the Joshua grove with her and sat leaning back against a tree, listening. He had a pretty amazing ear for a non-musician. Maybe it *was* all those grade school years playing that triangle, but he could always hear when she made a mistake. Even when he didn't know the piece of music she was playing.

The more she knew about him, the more she liked him. He still wasn't the kind of guy she would have looked at twice if she didn't know him. And if she hadn't been more or less forced to hang out with him because he was Stacy's boyfriend, they probably would have passed each other like ships in the night. But, the way things had happened, she'd gone beyond her first impression into really knowing him, and everything had changed.

It was ironic. After all the time she'd spent in Chicago hoping for a boyfriend, out here she'd found one right away. There were only two small problems: He was the guy her sister went with, and in a week she was going to have to leave him two thousand miles behind.

How far now?" she shouted to him over the rumble and rattle of the old VW as they sped along the desert highway.

"About ten miles off," he said. "But it's worth the drive!"

She pushed her seat back and put her feet up on the dash and leaned back and listened to Springsteen crackling out of the blue, lit radio. She looked ahead out the windshield. The darkness spread over the desert like a black drape. The headlights cut through it like lasers.

And then suddenly, off to the side, in the distance, there was a flickering of orange-yellow-white. A fire — far off, high up.

"Looks like the others beat us here," Sam said as he swung the car off the road and headed across the sandy ground. Jackrabbits skittered out of the headlight beams and the bumper snagged on a few tumbleweeds.

"We have to climb on foot from here," he said when they'd pulled to a stop amid all the other cars parked at the base of the mesa, which jutted straight up from the desert floor like a giant sand castle with a flat top. It was a steep climb, but Alix was in shape now and found she was barely winded when she reached the top.

It was quite a sight. The fire was huge. The night was a solid wall around it. It was like standing on a deserted stage in the center of a very bright spotlight. Most of the kids were dancing to a boom box tape deck set on a rock. Some were just sitting around. Rosalie was among these, sitting next to Mike.

She was touching up her eyeliner, using the mirror in her compact. And so at first she didn't see Alix. When she did, she nodded hello, but without smiling. And when she put her makeup away in her purse, got up and came over to where Alix was standing with Sam (but without The Arm, a habit she'd managed to gradually break him of).

"Stace," she said. "Can I talk to you for a sec?" Sam looked on with interest. He loved gossip more than any guy Alix had ever known.

"Uh," Rosalie said, speaking to Alix, but looking straight at Sam, "Alone."

He blinked and said. "Oh, I see. *Alone*. Well, in that case I think I'll just go over and have a little chat with Mike," he said, and walked away.

When the two girls were left alone, Rosalie motioned for Stacy to come over to the rocks near the edge of the mesa.

"You're not going to push me off, are you?" Alix teased.

"No. I want to thank you."

"Thank me? For insulting you?"

"No. For doing what good friends should do. Telling me the truth. I was trying to deny it, but the fact is that I've put on twenty pounds since ninth grade. I can't wear any of the clothes I have from back then. Still, I tried to kid myself it was really only five pounds and I could drop it whenever I wanted. Well, when you said that the other day, I'll admit I was steamed. But then I went home and thought about it, and I knew you were right. I was becoming a porker and Mike's wandering eye was leading him to Sonia Brown. You were just trying to save me from that, I realized. And I also saw that I had to take drastic action."

"Liposuction."

"No silly. A diet. I've been on 1,200 calories

166

a day for three weeks now. I've lost six and a half pounds. Can't you tell?"

Alix stood back and inspected Rosalie carefully, then said honestly, "No."

The two of them looked at each other for a long tense moment. Alix was the first to crack a smile and then Rosalie began laughing.

"You really are something, Wyatt," she said and gave Alix a play punch in the arm. This was Rosalie's greatest sign of friendship, a holdover from her tomboy days.

Mike and Sam wandered back over.

"Nobody stabbed anybody?" Mike said.

"Yeah," Sam said. "We were expecting some real tooth and nail action."

"Sorry to disappoint you boys, but we were making up," Alix said.

"That's right," Rosalie added, pulling out her compact and doing a quick check on her hair in the mirror. "Stacy gave me some constructive criticism, and I was mature enough to accept it. Which is the way best friends are with each other. So there will be no mudslinging for you weirdos to feast your eyes on. We are very civilized young women out here in the desert."

"In that case," Mike said, taking Rosalie's hand and pulling her off the rock where she'd been sitting. "Maybe I can take you away for a little dancing."

Alix and Sam watched them dance for a while. Rosalie and Mike were the best dancers in school. Alix, who, for all her musical ability, had two left feet on the dance floor, loved watching them. She loved being here tonight, loved being part of this crowd, even though they weren't really like her. There was still something warm and friendly and secure about having friends.

This was something that was missing in her life back in Chicago and she was determined — even though it would mean bursting through her shyness — that she was going to make friends in school next year. Her days as a loner were over.

Another part of feeling so happy being there was sitting next to Sam, just feeling close without even talking. She'd never been this close to a guy before. He'd become so open in talking to her and she loved that. But the more open he was with her, the more guilty she felt for not confiding in him. She still had one big secret that put a wall between them. More and more she had been wanting to smash that wall down and tonight she couldn't resist anymore.

"Sam?"

"Yeah?"

"I'm . . . I'm not the person you thought I was."

"Oh, I already know that," he said, brushing aside her bangs and kissing her forehead. "I never knew there were all these different sides to you that I've started to see this summer."

"No, I mean I'm really *not* who you think I am. I'm not Stacy. I'm Alix."

"Sure, Stace." Sam kissed the tip of her nose this time.

"Sam, listen! I'm *serious*!" Alix felt him pull away. For a moment she couldn't meet his eyes. When she did, they stared at each other for a long time.

Then Sam said, "It's true, isn't it? You *aren't* Stacy. You're . . . you're your *sister*?"

She nodded.

"Okay, *Alix*. What's going on?"

Quickly, she told him the whole story about the switch. She expected him to be mad at her, but all he did was shake his head.

"Boy," he said. At first it was all he said. Then he added, "I knew something was different, but I thought it was me. That my feelings about you were changing. Now I see that I'd just finally met the right twin for me."

He turned to look at her, and neither of them said anything for a long time. Finally he asked, "What are we going to do?"

Alix shook her head.

"I don't know. I really don't know."

Chapter 18

Alix's plane came into Chicago from the west, then circled over the lake. She could feel her heartbeat speed up a little. She was going home.

Stacy was waiting at the gate with Martine and their dad. Everybody gave Alix hugs and she felt so happy at being back that she almost forgot she wasn't supposed to be coming home, just visiting from California. For a little while longer she had to stay Stacy.

As soon as they all got back to the apartment, Alix dragged her sister into the bedroom and shut the door behind them. Both of them collapsed onto the beds, laughing at no one particular joke, just exhilarated at the great wonderful absurdity of pulling off the switch.

"We did it!" Alix said.

"There were a couple of moments I was sure

we were going to get caught, but we *didn't!*"
Stacy said, then cackled gleefully.

"I don't know about you," Alix said, "but
suddenly I'm *dying* to be me."

Stacy nodded eagerly.

"Me, too. Let's switch clothes now. Then
when we go back out, we can just be
ourselves."

"Not that it was so bad being you," Stacy
said as she pulled off Alix's striped boat neck
cotton top and gave it to her. "Pretty weird,
but it was never dull."

"I know. Whatever else happens in our lives,
I don't think either of us will ever forget this
summer," Alix said, stepping out of Stacy's
faded-to-white jeans. "Now, we'd better do a
quick de-briefing. Is there anything we need
to tell each other?"

"Well, I guess I have to let you know. I spent
your emergency fund."

"You didn't!"

"It was for a good cause, though," Stacy said
and explained about Brendan and his mother
and the dinner.

"Well, I guess I can't be too mad," Alix said.
"Now what else should I know?"

"Well, try to keep a straight face if it comes
up, but Martine's planning to name the baby
either Horace or Edwina."

Alix fell onto the bed she was laughing so hard.

"Good thing I told you now. Now, what should *I* know?"

"You got an A in geometry."

"I did!" Stacy squealed with delight and jumped up and down and then hugged Alix.

"*And* I think Mom's going to marry Alan."

Stacy nodded as though she suspected as much, and said, "That's a good thing, don't you think?"

"I guess so," Alix said. "I mean he's so nice and she's so happy. But it does kind of kill my fantasy about our old family getting back together."

"Sometimes you have to get new fantasies," Stacy said.

"I guess," Alix said.

Stacy said, "Here are a couple of other things . . ." She went on to tell how their father had discovered that Professor Faraci was away and that Alix hadn't been going to her Impressionist lectures. "They've really gotten behind you being a regular teen-age girl. Oh, and you now run a little."

"But I *do* run a little now!"

"Alix the Wimp?"

"Two miles a day," Alix said smugly.

"Hey. I'm impressed. Listen, after dinner I'll

take you over to meet your boyfriend." Stacy used all her acting skills to make this sound lighthearted, like it was no big deal that she was turning Brendan over to Alix. Even though it was the *last* thing in the world she wanted to do. Still, it was what she'd promised, and she tried to always keep her promises.

"Oh, great," Alix said, using her acting skills to sound excited about this new boyfriend even though she had exactly the boyfriend she wanted — back in Joshua Tree, California.

"Dinner!" shouted Martine. "Stacy?"

"Yes!" shouted both twins.

"Alix?"

"Coming!" they both yelled. And then chased each other out of the bedroom laughing.

Dinner was two huge bags their dad brought back from a Mexican restaurant. They all opened the cartons and foil plates and passed around napkins and forks and cans of soda.

"Boy, a real fiesta!" said Alix (the real Alix just being herself).

"Yeah, but if you want the best Mexican food, you have to come to California," said Stacy (the real Stacy just being herself).

They were both feeling relief at not having to play roles anymore. The switch had been great — and some pretty terrific stuff had happened to both of them because of it — but basically they were glad to be back in their own personalities.

"It's been so long since we've seen you, Stacy," Martine said.

Not as long as you think, thought Stacy as she spooned some refried beans and rice onto her plate.

"And we hear you passed geometry," her dad said.

"Passed it?" Stacy said. "I got an A."

"Wow," said Martine. "And we never thought you'd be able to get that stuff through your skull."

This stopped the conversation in its tracks for a moment until Steve started grinning affectionately at Martine.

"Would you like to take your foot out of your mouth before you start eating, dear?"

Everyone cracked up, including Martine, who also blushed.

"I'm just impossible, I know," she said. "I don't know how you all put up with me."

Even Alix could see that this was true, and that Martine probably didn't mean any harm by a lot of the goofy things she said.

"Could you pass me that avocado dip?" Martine said now. "I've got distinct avocado cravings."

"Must be little Englebert," Alix said.

"Horace," said Martine, but she didn't seem insulted. She knew everyone thought her names for the baby were awful, and so teased Alix back. "But now that you mention it, Englebert might be nice, too."

"Ooooo, what have I done?" Alix moaned, and everyone laughed and she knew things were going to be friendlier around here for her than they had been. Not to mention richer, what with all the baby-sitting money she was going to rake in.

After dinner, the twins went out together to meet Brendan.

"He said he'd be in the park at seven," Stacy told Alix.

"Should you be you and me be me, or should I be you and you be me?" Alix wondered.

"I guess I'd better be you for this first time at least. Then tonight I can fill you in on all the details about him so you'll be able to fool him." Stacy hoped the deadness in her heart wasn't coming through in her voice.

"Is that him?" Alix said, pointing at a gorgeous runner going by.

"Al. That guy is incredibly good looking, a major jock, *and* about twenty-five years old. I said I'd get you a boyfriend, not Tom Cruise!" And then, turning the other way, she saw him coming, and pointed him out to her sister. "*That's* Brendan."

"Him? He's skinnier than I am. And his ears stick out."

"How superficial can you be? Going on looks alone like that. And if one more person mentions his ears to me, I'm going to have to strangle them."

"I'm sorry," Alix said. "You're right. I'm jumping to conclusions. I'm sure he's a fascinating person."

"Yabba dabba doo," he said as he approached them. Of course, Stacy knew this sounded idiotic to Alix, who didn't know how much the two of them loved old "Flintstones" reruns. And then it came tumbling in on her all the hundreds of private jokes she and Brendan now had between them. How was she ever going to explain all these to Alix. And did she even want to?

"This is my sister, Stacy," Stacy said.

"Just in from our westernmost state," he said, then offered his hand. "Your sister's told me a lot about you. I hear you passed geometry."

"Yeah," Alix said, finding it kind of funny to be impersonating Stacy when she was standing right there. "Even we jocks can sometimes wrap our minds around a few numbers." Then, for good measure, she dropped to the ground and did a few push-ups, the way Stacy herself did when she was trying to burn off a little excess energy.

When Stacy saw what Alix was doing, she burst out laughing. Of course, Brendan was mystified. He threw up his hands.

"I've heard all about how weird twins are, but I'm telling you two, if you get weird on me, I'll get weirder — I'll go home and get on my radio and call my interplanetary friends to come rescue me."

Stacy laughed and grabbed him by the neck and shouted toward the sky. "Come and get this boy! He's too strange for this planet anyway!"

The three of them went down to Navy Pier, where there was going to be a big Labor Day free rock concert. They had fun all night, just acting goofy, and Alix wound up really liking Brendan. But what she liked best of all was how great he and Stacy were together. He definitely brought out the best in her sister. They belonged together. But how was she going to make Stacy see that? How was she going to stop her in the middle of her big plan to give Brendan away?

She waited until late that night when they were lying in the old twin beds they'd gotten when their parents put their cribs away years and years ago. It was dark and silent except for the city noises drifting up through the open window.

"Stace?"

"Mmmm?" She sounded asleep.

"Can I talk to you for a minute? It's kind of important."

Alix waited until Stacy rolled over and propped herself sleepily up on an elbow.

"Shoot," said Stacy.

"It's about Brendan."

"You like him?"

"Yeah, I do. But for *you*."

"For *me*?"

"Yeah. I know you think he's perfect for me, but the truth is, he's perfect for you." Alix cleared her throat and waited.

Stacy sighed.

"I know. It's true. I found him for you, but then I couldn't help liking him myself. Are you mad?"

"Not at all." Alix felt like cheering with relief, but she kept her tone casual. "It's great seeing you so happy with someone."

"Yeah. I wish I was that happy with my *real* boyfriend."

"Sam?"

"Mmmhmm. I can't say I'm overexcited about going back to him."

"Well . . ." Alix tried to phrase this as delicately as she could. "I can't say *I'm* overexcited about leaving him."

"Alix!" Stacy shouted, if shouts could be whispered. She turned on the light on the night table between them to see her sister grinning sheepishly.

"What can I say?"

"You sly dog! Falling for my boyfriend. I thought he wasn't your type?"

"He isn't. That's the crazy thing. But still. . . . And, Stacy, I told him about the switch."

"You *did*?"

"It just got to a point where I had to."

"What did he say? What *happened*?"

"Well . . . he took it very well, I must say."

Stacy grinned at Alix. "You mean he decided he liked Alix, and not Alix-as-Stacy, right?"

Alix nodded.

"So," said Stacy. "Do you want to go back to California instead of me? Keep pretending to Mom and Dad?"

"No . . . no, that's too crazy. We'd go nuts. I think we have to take back our own lives, *and* the guys we like. Even though the geography's all wrong, at least the emotions will be right. You should tell Brendan and we'll just have to have long-distance boyfriends in addition to long-distance twins."

"And there are always letters, phone calls, vacations . . ."

"Right."

"Maybe it'll work. And for sure, I'll feel better once I've told Brendan. He's always known I have a secret and now I can tell him. But let's not ever tell anyone else about the switch, okay? I'd rather it stay as much just between us as possible."

"Fine by me," Stacy said. "I don't think anyone else even suspects."

They were having breakfast the next morning, as themselves, when the phone rang. Alix ran and got it.

"Gram!" Then she turned to Stacy and said, "Quick! Get on the bedroom extension."

"So . . ." Gram said when both twins were on the line. "How'd your summers go?"

"Great," said Stacy.

"Great," agreed Alix.

"I am referring to your *especially interesting* summers, of course," Gram said, and then paused meaningfully.

"Gram!" Stacy said from the bedroom phone.

"You knew?" Alix whispered into the receiver.

"Don't think you're the only twins to have had the idea," Gram told them. "Although I don't think many twin switches have been quite so outrageous!"

"You knew!" Alix repeated.

"All along!" Stacy said.

Gram's hearty laughter came to them all the way from Missouri. "Land's sakes! Don't you girls know by now that you can never fool another twin!"

About the Author

CAROL STANLEY has written fifteen books for young adults, most recently, *Second Best Sister*. She grew up in Michigan and now lives in Chicago, where she is currently at work on another book. Ms. Stanley is also a swimmer, a runner, and the proud owner of Sebastian, "cutest dog in the world."

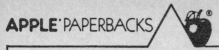